NEW LIGHT

Warren Doten

NEW LIGHT

WARREN DOTSON

NEW DEGREE PRESS

NEW LIGHT

ISBN   978-1-63676-806-9   *Paperback*
         978-1-63730-236-1   *Kindle Ebook*
         978-1-63730-249-1   *Ebook*

CONTENTS

———

WARREN DOTSON:
AUTHOR'S NOTE

———

To give an idea of what exactly I'm creating, I'll explain where the inspiration for this story started. In 2007, I first played a game known as *Kingdom Hearts*. The game is characterized as having an incredible combination of characters from *Final Fantasy* and Disney. The two on paper sound like they don't mesh, with *Final Fantasy* being about the consequences of messing with the planet and Disney being about magic and escapism, but they did. In fact, to this day, the concept has performed so well it continues to have new titles and stories made. The story would fill me with anticipation as the saga continued.

It was those moments before that I wanted to emulate in this story. The giddiness and excitement would be hammered with incredible anxiousness as I kept thinking about the story unfolding before me. My mind would race while playing or even just watching the game. Who would show up? Who would be a main character? Who was powerful enough to impose their will? These questions plagued me, and I loved the joy of discovering the answers as I kept going. This combination of magic and unpredictability always stuck with me and, after a few tries at making something that could be in that style, I found it in this book.

The purpose of this book is to be a reprieve from the world and a way of taking a step back and enjoying something without having to be overwhelmed with everything happening. While the novel does feature moments where it will seem like a reflection of what is currently taking place, more precisely the world will share the issue of prejudice and hierarchy; however, it is meant to be an escape and a chance to enjoy the stories of other people trying to do what is right.

I feel I always need a way to do that every day or I'll crash and burn immediately. These characters will be like most people you meet and know; they're characters you can relate to and latch on to. They're meant to put a smile on your face when you see them, like finding your favorite person whenever you need a pick-me-up. With this book, people won't spend all their time having a heart attack or being incredibly upset. You will get to laugh and have fun imagining a world that takes great leaps beyond anything we do while showcasing a new type of world.

The book is also about adding something missing to the genre of fantasy with a fully POC cast. I do love reading novels, but whenever I want to read fiction or talk about epic stories in fantasy worlds, I never see myself there. I'm a black man, and I can't think of many black wizards, let alone very many black protagonists who appear in the fiction stories I grew up reading. The closest I remember relating to a character was when one would have a quirk I share, not the same skin tone.

Whenever I do think of POC characters in science fiction literature, they are either a background character, an example, or "other." With this story, I'll take that notion and completely dismantle it by finally adding a few black wizards. People of color won't feel like they don't exist in fantasy.

I write more for myself than anything else; though, if I can, I want to show how to create a more representative canon. I was a kid who had interests that went against those of my peers and even if the books I read weren't for everyone or known by everyone, they were the books I needed.

Those stories helped me find my ambitions, goals, and joys, and I loved getting to know the characters in those stories more than anything else. This story is going to be a realization of what those stories added to and created for me. This is my story, my voice, and my imagination on display.

The biggest hope is that this will be a new step for imaginative fiction. Building a new narrative for POC writers and storytellers from black to Asian to Latino. This book's team will add more perspectives to a genre many of my friends growing up defined as stagnant for years. These characters aren't bland; they have problems, emotions, and fears people have all the time. For many, they will see themselves at the forefront, talking and working to fix the problems presented. They'll finally get a chance to be a part of the narrative. Their roles and purposes are still being found in themselves, and they'll go up against tough competition as they face challenges. They will read this book and finally get a sense they can and do exist in these stories and environments. These groups are not a one-to-one representation.

This is a story for fans of the idea of what happens when the mystic and magical combines with how the future looks and what it can do. Fans of science fiction can read this and find a world evolved beyond our own present. Fantasy fans can see a world where the magical is created in a unique and stylized way—where being a Mage can also reveal a part of who you are.

This is a story for those who love adventures. This book is epic, this book is grand, and this book is something more than just a run-of-the-mill protagonist story. Every character will give someone something to enjoy and something new to talk about.

CHAPTER 1

DEPARTURE

———

A young Mystic sat on her rock with the best view of the sunrise that made the sky a pastel painting of oranges, yellows, and pinks. Looking over the sea adjacent to her home, her heart ached with joy. She had been blessed with opportunity. Her life was now going to be lived. The birthmark on her back, signifying her Mage type, was glowing. The extended angel wings shone greatly as her body reacted to the nerves and excitement welling up. Her overwhelming sense of joy was nearly uncontainable. She was ecstatic. Her name was Zhang Mei, but she preferred Med. Her Mage type: Dark Angel—the shadowed cousin of a Light Angel.

Med loved her home and wouldn't change the idea of growing up there for anything; however, she wanted to experience things beyond just a house on the beach and a town near the shore. She was determined to find good use of her abilities. She healed people by shifting the pain. Healing was the only magical technique she had been taught. She had received no training on how to manipulate reality or how to become a more powerful person, and she didn't understand why she couldn't do that but never bothered to ask out of anxiety.

She learned about her abilities from a report from a Mystic. This Mystic had witnessed Med use her powers while visiting Soliopolis. When she was three, she suffered a small cut on her knee. After a touch of her hand over the wound, Med was able to heal the wound. This caught the eye of the Mystic, who reported it to the head of all Mystic Operations and true Sorceress of Mystian, Solaria. Med heard everything about her growing up but had never met her. The idea of Solaria was incredible and awe-inspiring. She was Med's end goal to become as much of a Mage/Non-Mage Cooperation advocate as her idol who was her opposite: a Light Angel.

Med wanted to ask her so much about what her powers meant and what her title of Dark Angel held. Med sat on her rock, staring at the same waves that beat upon the sand on the shore. *Home is nice, but I feel like I'll never do anything just sitting here.* She let the thoughts sit for a minute and then got up to grab her bags. She was off to her new home, Complex 50 site 3.23, one of the many bases for Mystics. Med had been adamant that she wanted to work somewhere other than Soliopolis for her Mystic assignment; an opportunity not all Mages wanted nor was expected. Many Mages were overwhelmed by the expectation to move up to Sage and one day become a Sorcerer or Sorceress, the two being some of the highest positions in their society.

Med walked into the quaint little living room with the aroma of candles and stocked shelves of books. She took a few looks around before picking up her duffle bag and bringing it over to a waiting car outside. She looked at her dad's favorite spot on the couch to watch television and her mom's spot to work. She took one last glance before throwing a small backpack over her shoulder and picking up the huge sack.

She walked out of her house and headed over to her parents. She gave them both a hug and a reassuring smile.

"Call us when you make it there, okay, sweetie?" Her mom held Med's hands.

"Don't worry, Mom. I'll make sure to do that." Med walked over to the car and opened the door. She looked back one last time and waved.

The car left for the airport. Along the way, Med looked from the car window at Soliopolis. She saw the local farmers taking to the fields. They bent down to take care of the seeds while the automated tractors scanned for pests lurking in the plants. Further down, she saw a group of children playing in a small park phasing through walls to avoid being tagged. All the while, the radio told a different story from hers.

The story was about the prodigies of Mystian with the reader rattling off names like Cyset and Jacks wildly and the expectations put on them. Med was not considered a prodigy—more "precious cargo." She didn't bask in the glory of being a talented Dark Angel. Her life stayed hidden from the popular world and was spent with only a few visitors.

A hidden power not thrust into the light like most, she was not blasted with the heat of the spotlight but left more to sprout in the sun. In another environment, some Mages were well-known for their magic ability.

The radio blasted, saying Solaria's protégé, Drake Celeste, was looking forward to being a Mystic. "At nineteen years of age, the young prodigy is one of few Wind Wizards in existence as some much like..."

The radio cut off. Med shrugged; a quiet car ride was fine by her. She figured the driver wasn't trying to make her too anxious by making a common gesture so younger Mystics didn't unleash magic due to stress. There wasn't a very long silence before she found herself in an exchange with her chaperone.

"So, you, uh, excited?" the driver asked.

"Yeah," said Med. "I'm very excited. Not many people around here get to do something like this." Looking out at all the mom-and-pop shops, her hometown wasn't just quaint, it was tranquility personified; but when you're an eighteen-year-old, that's not your most preferred option. Her home was infectious. Soliopolis was a great place to remain if you wished to be unbothered. Outside the citizens simply walked around content with what they had. Their day-to-day routines were simple and comfortable. They felt at ease knowing what was around and were unbothered with a plethora of issues every day or so.

Med wasn't meant for that. She felt inclined to do something amazing as a Mage with such a unique ability. Even the thought of not doing anything left her with a knot in her stomach. She was determined to do something great and expand her world beyond the fog of unknowing.

Med's eyes shifted through the green fields beyond the small town as she began to approach the airport. The image of the tarmac filled her head and began to build her anxiety. She was giddy at the thought of leaving home, but the giddiness became anxiety at the thought of being left alone in a world she had only been told about.

Everything she knew had been told to her by people who were supposed to teach her. They taught her how to defend herself, communicate, and how to use her magic. Though they never gave her a full picture of every detail, she believed them. It was her only choice.

The car took a turn into the access tunnel leading to the tarmac. Driving through, Med grabbed her bag and got ready to step out of the car. Med was awestruck at the sight of a private jet waiting. Sleek, elegant, and painted with bright gold lines, it was immaculate. She exited the car with her mouth agape and her mind blown. She couldn't find words.

She boarded the plane from the ladder and took in the beauty of it: the leather seats, the windows, the dim yet heavenly lighting. Her eyes were being spoiled with the sight of luxury. Interrupted by a tap on the shoulder, she turned, and standing before her was the Sorceress of Mystian, Solaria.

"Hello, Med. It's nice to finally meet you," she said.

Med was awestruck. She was standing before her idol, in a private jet, and being told she was the anticipated guest. She looked at Solaria, who stood at seven feet tall and walked with the elegance of a celestial swan. Her power radiated with a visible energy glow around her.

Med finally mustered out a sentence. "I, um, hello, ma'am."

Solaria simply gave a smile.

"Please, take a seat," Solaria said. "It's more comfortable to fly that way, and we don't want to be late. Nexi Sciene Airport can be pretty busy at any point of the day."

Med took a seat, processing how in the world any of this was happening as the plane taxied over to the runway. As it did, Med looked at a file on the table and picked it up.

"Those will be your teammates," Solaria said.

Med flipped it open and saw the first face. A young man, nineteen years old, dark-skinned with dreads going down his neck. In his photo, he was smiling with a prideful look.

"Jackson Byron, or Jacks," Med read aloud.

"Heir to the Byron fortune after he's done being a Mystic."

Med flipped through to the next page. This time, a girl also nineteen, with dark hair and blue streaks, was pale and looking away from the camera.

"Bella Breakrow. Shade."

Med continued to the next page. This girl looked tough, with tan skin and long, slightly red hair. She was smiling, freckled, and muscled.

"Dixie Planina." Med paused. "There's not another name here."

Solaria nodded. "Funnily enough, Dixie does not have a Mage name like most."

Med turned to the next page. A scruffy guy in the picture had his face covered in dirt, shaggy hair, and a smile showing jagged and chipped teeth.

"Steven. Scratch. Where's his last name?" Med asked.

"Oh, he doesn't have one," Solaria said.

"He doesn't?" Med looked back at the page.

"Well, he was raised by coyotes in the desert."

Med shook her head as she tried to process what she just heard. She shook it off and turned the page to the last member. Drake Celeste. She knew him; Solaria's protege. His skin was like Jacks', eyes with bright yellow irises, the mark of a Wind Wizard, and hair cut high with a fade. Face focused and eyes driven, his portrait said enough about him.

She didn't need to speak his name to get an answer. She put down the folder and felt herself jerk back as the plane went down the runway. She experienced takeoff for the first time and gripped the sides of the chair tightly as the plane climbed into the clouds. As the plane leveled out, Med loosened her grip little by little with shaking arms. As she relaxed, she looked up to see Solaria offering her a cup of tea. Med thanked her and took it.

"Well, Med, may I ask how you liked growing up in Soliopolis?" Solaria asked.

Med took a sip before answering. "Oh, I, well, it wasn't terrible. Just incredibly boring."

"Yes, I guess that would make sense. Soliopolis isn't exactly a place of much excitement, but that's a bit of a fault on my end," Solaria said.

"Your end?" Med asked.

"You see, I'm made aware of Mages who are gifted with magical abilities or traits since their birth."

"You knew who I was the minute I was born?"

"Yes," Solaria said. "Due to your registration, I thought it would be better if you were placed somewhere there wasn't exactly a huge problem of extreme distrust or unrest."

Med's mind raced. Should she be extremely angry, should she wonder why this was such a big deal, or should she simply nod? All she wanted was an answer to a single question. "Why?"

Solaria manifested a globe in her hand. "Do you recognize the places on this globe?"

"Yes. This is Mystian."

"You know how Mages live in our world?" Solaria asked as she made the globe spin.

"Yes," Med said. "We chose to hold back certain abilities as a compromise. For example, Fire Rats don't keep stoves in their homes because they can heat food."

"Now, with that reestablished, I can better answer why, at this moment in time, we are experiencing quite a surge in unexplained energy," Solaria said, putting the globe down on the table between them.

"Unexplained?" Med shifted in her seat.

"Energy, more or less, uncontrollable or unfound for a long time, is not entirely unheard of, but it could be a very big issue if unchecked."

"Am I going to be part of the response to all of this?" Med asked.

"To be quite frank, I don't want to send Mystics to handle something this extreme. I'd rather handle it through conversation, but I don't feel I have the choice at the moment," Solaria said. "Which is why I've added you."

"I don't think I understand," Med replied. "Why me?"

"You see, you and your other teammates will be Sorcerers and Sorceresses in the future." Solaria took a breath. "I would like to see a more informed group of leaders in the future, those from quiet places, big cities, nowhere, and the most notable areas."

Med thought about what was being said and found herself feeling calm hearing these words directly from Solaria. This didn't feel like she had no choice and no idea, but a chance—so with a very clear thought, Med came to a decision.

"I'll do whatever I can. I want nothing more than to be a Mystic who can help keep her world safe," Med answered proudly and confidently, making sure it was clear how much she believed in the cause.

Solaria smiled at the proud new Mystic and put a hand on her shoulder. "I am happy to see such conviction, but I do want you to be warned: Mages and Mystics are not celebrities, so whatever you do, find a way to look at the world with hope and find people to stand with you."

Med nodded and felt at ease. Her lifelong work of training had paid off and was now beginning to take shape.

She took the things Solaria said with a very simple thought of what may happen next but didn't let any of it keep her from being excited about the next part of her journey.

CHAPTER 2

EXERCISE

———

New home, same guy. That was the mindset of Cyset, a Wind Wizard and protégé of Solaria. He had been gearing up to be a Mystic his whole life. He was focused and his mind sharp. The only thing he needed was to figure out his new room layout. He was living in a small bedroom with limited space. All he had was a desk, a small walk-in closet, a bit of wall room, and his imagination.

"All right, I've got a bit more room on my desk, a good spot for a photo," Cyset said, placing it on the furniture and looking at it for a bit. His mind stopped worrying about the room when he felt a presence. He swung around and looked into the face of his longtime friend and training partner, Jacks.

Jacks simply shrugged it off and looked at his friend like he was daydreaming. "Hey, Breeze Head. You still in the realm of Mystian?"

Cyset shoved his friend jokingly. "Got a lot of nerve doing that, Fireball. I can spin you like a top if you're not careful." He waved his fingers. He put down a few more items on the desk and bed before leaning against the wall and letting out a small sigh.

"Hey, come on, this is what we've been waiting for, right? The chance to break out and do our own thing?" Jacks asked.

"Yeah, of course. This is what I've always wanted to do, but it's a little overwhelming."

"Oh, overwhelming!" called Shade from the other side of the door. "I just got used to the whole thing about moving into a new home and you want to say this is overwhelming, mister trained-for-this-all-his-life."

Cyset had just met Shade but could already tell she was not used to the thought of being selected. "Look, it's not like what I imagined, you know. I expected something like less a college dorm and more military barrack. Something bleak, or more firehouse." He shrugged. He had always imagined a very structured building with less wallpaper and more simple drywall.

"Come on, man, you know this is pretty sweet. At least you don't have to share a room with somebody," Jacks said.

Cyset shook his head. He wasn't too opposed to enjoying what was going on, but he wasn't jumping up and down with an extreme overabundance of joy at his new situation. He readjusted and looked at his friend.

"Can you go to the kitchen so the new guy doesn't go nuts?" Jacks said.

Cyset shook his head and walked out of his room. Before he got down the hall, Jacks grabbed him.

"Speaking of which, what about the whole… you know?" Jacks asked.

Cyset sighed. "You mean having a Dark Angel on the team?"

Jacks nodded.

"Look, I say we just take it one step at a time, all right?" Cyset rubbed his head.

Jacks shrugged. Cyset continued over to the small living area and kitchen. He looked over to his right inside the kitchen where Scratch stood, staring intensely at the coffee machine. He was sniffing it, almost stalking it as though he was trying to figure out when to pounce on it.

"Scratch, you all right, man?" Cyset asked.

Scratch raised his hand signaling him not to move or make a sound. "I'm still trying to see what it will do," Scratch said, keeping his eyes trained on the coffee maker.

"Those uh, coyotes, didn't tell you what a coffee maker was, did they?" Cyset asked, scratching his head. He turned to Jacks. He shook his head, chuckling at the whole raised-by-coyotes concept. It was crazy but deserved some belief given Animal Magicians could communicate with animals.

Before the two could try and explain the idea to him further, they heard the door open. In walked another member of the team. Cyset started examining her, looking for her mark and finding it on her hugely muscled right arm. A green rock—a Dirt Driver's mark. He started putting a tally in his mind. *All right, so, I control the wind, Jacks brings the heat, and she can move the earth. If we ever get a Typhoon Tamer, we'll have all the elements down.*

He put on his best face, stood up, and walked over. Extending his hand, he said, "Hello. I take it you're Dixie?"

"Right as rain, friend," Dixie said. "I take it I'm at Complex 50 site 3.23 or however you say it."

Cyset thought the name was long-winded, but it made sure there was no confusion between other Mystic complexes. "That would be the one. I'm Drake Celeste, better known as Cyset, your team leader. Let me introduce you to everyone. Over there is my best friend, Mr. Jackson Byron or Jacks, a Fire Rat."

Jacks gave a two-fingered salute from his position.

Cyset rolled his eyes and pointed to the counter. "Over there, the fellow stalking our coffee machine, is Scratch. He's an Animal Magician."

Scratch turned his head and waved with a big smile on his face.

"So, I'm stuck with all guys?" Dixie asked.

"Nah. Shade's in the back getting used to all of her stuff," Jacks said.

"Shade?" Dixie asked.

"Shade's a Shadow User and part of our team. She's from Nexi Sciene itself," Cyset said.

"Oh, is that so?" Dixie asked. "By the way, why the second names?"

"You mean our Mage names?" Jacks asked.

Dixie looked puzzled at the thought of it. Cyset was just puzzled at the idea of someone not having a Mage name despite being a Mage. "You know, the name that defines your character as a Mage," he explained. "Like I was born at sunset and I'm a Wind Wizard, so I combined Cyclone and Sunset, getting 'Cyset.'"

"So, why 'Jacks' for you?" Dixie asked.

"Oh, that's easy," Jacks said. "I chose it because it sounds cool. Why can't that just be a thing?"

Cyset chuckled as his friend made his case. Out of the corner of his eye, he saw Shade enter the room.

"I chose 'Shade' because it's a nice little play on shadow," she said.

"Well, I'm just Dixie. Pleasure to meet you, Shade," Dixie said.

"Same to you," Shade said.

Cyset smiled. It was nice to talk to other Mages about stuff like this.

"So, I heard there were six of us. Where's member six?" Shade asked, looking around.

Damn it, I was really hoping I wouldn't have to explain this. "That's a little tricky," Cyset said.

"Tricky or classified?" Dixie asked.

"Yes," Cyset replied.

"Oh, boy, here we go," Jacks said.

"Member six is from somewhere slightly more isolated, so she'll have to be met personally and brought in secret to avoid a media circus," Cyset explained.

"How much of a media circus? More than all of the radio chatter about you and the prince over there?" Shade said, nodding toward Jacks.

"Yes, even more of a media circus because Non-Mages aren't exactly chomping at the bit to hear there will be more Mystics around," Jacks said.

"Why? We're the good guys," Scratch said.

Cyset and Jacks looked at each other. He jerked his head at Jacks, signaling him not to make a scene.

"Point is…" Cyset paused to think of his answer. He didn't want to be too overdramatic. "She's from a quiet place, and it's better for her to get eased into things, you know?"

"I'll take your word for it," Dixie said.

Shade raised an eyebrow but said nothing. At that moment, a ding sounded.

"Ah!" Scratch yelled.

Cyset turned his head to see what was going on. He saw Scratch observing the machine as it started pouring out coffee.

"Oh, *that's* what it does," he said.

Cyset chuckled as he watched his teammate observing the coffee maker with such an intrigued face. He was just happy everything was starting off so well.

"This will work," he whispered to himself, crossing his arms.

CHAPTER 3

FIRST IMPRESSION

———

Med felt herself shake as she gazed at the complex. It was like staring down a fortress. A consolidated hub to house a unit of Mystics, the building was huge and powerful, holding her gaze as she studied it. She gulped heavily as she tried to find some calm and stoicism inside of herself.

Solaria put a hand on her shoulder and gave her a reassuring nod. Med returned it and readied herself as she prepared for what came next. *You asked for this. Just be ready for anything.*

A yellow muscle car, a glowing scarlet speedster, a sleek raven black motorcycle, and an older but refurbished truck were lined up in a row. They were beautiful.

"Hmm. I guess he made some adjustments to his car after all," Solaria said.

"Who?" Med asked.

"Cyset. His car is the yellow one." Solaria pointed.

"Cyset built that?"

"Oh, yes. That's how he bonded with Jacks," Solaria said as she continued ahead. Med followed her up to the door that led inside to a sitting area where the others were. "Are you ready to meet your peers?"

Med nodded while her insides entangled. She wanted to jump up and down with excitement. *So cool. So, so cool!*

The door opened to the living room where the group was settled. She hadn't gotten a chance to hang around other Mages her age growing up, so to do it now was a great change. The isolation she had felt all her life was starting to disappear. They were not meditative mentors—they were people like her.

She scanned the room in awe as Solaria walked forward.

"Looks like you've made yourselves at home," Solaria said.

Jacks and Shade bowed their heads. Dixie seemed to stand still while Scratch stood at attention, but out of the corner of her eye, she noticed someone simply nodding at all of the pageantries the others were giving and shrugging toward Solaria. She was trying to place how nonchalant he could be in Solaria's presence until it hit her: that was Cyset. *That's Solaria's protégé.* She kept her eyes focused on the group as Solaria continued speaking.

"Please, don't be so formal. It's a short visit," Solaria said. The Mystics stood at ease. "I came to explain the expected goals and help introduce the newest member." She turned to Med and nodded for her to come forward. Med waved to the people in the room.

"Hello. My name is Zhang Mei, but I believe it's better you call me Med," she said. Saying this for the first time to a group was anxiety-inducing. She could be judged or even rejected for her abilities. Her fear was also met with relief as she was able to speak around Mages her age. "I am a Dark Angel." The fear in her body lightened as no one showed fear. Instead, they showed interest. Interest not in the ability but in her. There were no feelings or looks of anything except curiosity.

"She'll be of great use to this group. As a Dark Angel, she'll be able to give a very obvious minority a voice," Solaria said. "Given why we've paired you all together, you'll need her more than you think."

"What comes next?" Jacks asked.

"To put it simply," Solaria said, "you are a new type of team. We've chosen people from different backgrounds and environments; hopefully to end the issue of Mystics themselves feeling underrepresented. I won't lie to you—there will be push-back; however, this team is more important than making calls or talking to a man in a suit. This will be considered incredibly unorthodox but I see it as a perfect solution."

Her words struck a chord with Med as she felt a surge of her energy grow around her. She understood everything and nodded. Her peers nodded as well, hooked by the words. As soon as she finished speaking, Solaria flashed a bright light and disappeared.

When the glow faded from the room. Med searched for Solaria. She was not alone in her confusion. Scratch and Shade looked up, down, and all around for her.

"How in the hell did she do that?" Shade asked.

"Don't look at me, my magic isn't based in creation, it's based on genetic manipulation," Scratch said.

Med stared at the spot Solaria had been with her mouth agape. She tried to put together where Solaria could have gone.

"That's a new one. Med, right?" Cyset asked as Med looked up.

She froze. *Okay, just introduce yourself. It's fine. Don't say anything stupid.* "Oh, yeah, Med. That's me."

"Nice to meet you. Drake Celeste. Call me Cyset."

She shook his hand and thought she was okay but was then met with another face.

"Jackson Byron. You can call me Jacks." Jacks offered his hand.

Med spoke after gaining her breath. "N-nice to meet both of you. I'm sorry, you startled me a little. I've never been surrounded by so much 'positive' attention."

The two looked at each other and shrugged.

A tall girl with light brown hair extended her hand to her. "Uh, hi, I'm Med," she said.

"Nice to meet ya. Dixie," Dixie said with a nod.

Med took her hand and shook it out a little. Dixie had a firmer handshake than the other two but still a warm welcome.

"Hey, why don't I show you back to your room?" Dixie said, edging her along.

Med followed her to the girls' side of the complex. Med walked up to her room with a nice open space. It was more spread out with a bed, an area to stretch, and a closet.

"It's not a lot, but it looks peaceful, huh?" said Dixie.

"This'll be perfect," Med said.

"Really?" Dixie tilted her head.

"Yeah. I mean, it'll take some work, but I'll give it a shot." Med nodded.

"I understand perfectly," Shade said, standing in the hallway with her arms folded. Med turned to see her postured up and confident. "Bella. Everyone just calls me Shade."

"Med."

"This your first time being in a place like this?" Shade asked.

"Yes," Med said. *Wow, this feels like a lot.*

"Well, don't worry. You'll get used to it almost immediately." Shade walked away.

Med set her duffle bag on the floor and took in the room.

"I'll leave ya to it," Dixie said. "You get yourself settled and everything, okay?"

"Yeah, thank you," Med said as Dixie walked off too. Med laid down on the bed and closed her eyes, letting the atmosphere of the base overtake her and get into her mind as she collapsed into this new world. The feeling of being in a new environment spread quickly but her moment was disrupted by a knock at the door.

"Hello?" a voice called.

"Eek!" she screamed before readjusting herself.

"Oh, sorry! I gotta learn not to do that," Scratch said, hanging from her door.

Med held her chest as if her soul would jump out if she didn't. "No, it's... it's okay. I, uh, It's nice to meet you."

"Oh, I'm Scratch, an Animal Magician from the desert." He jumped down.

"Nice to meet you, I'm Med," she said as she examined him.

"How you feeling so far?" Scratch asked.

"Um, a little overwhelmed, but I think I'll get used to it," Med said.

"Neat. Do you have a plan for what you are going to do here?" Scratch asked.

"I'm going to, uh..." Med paused. His fast pace of speaking was getting to her. She hadn't fully thought about a designated goal; more of a purpose she wanted to find with her work in the world. "I'm going to do whatever I can."

"Cool, I'll leave you to getting set up just wanted to say hi all right see ya," Scratch said, bouncing down the hall and off to his room.

Med shook her head and rubbed it, trying to let whatever just happened to sink in.

She got used to her new room quickly. The space was fine for her and the serenity was nice. She laid down looking up at the ceiling. *You asked for this, so now you're here. What would you consider your next step, Med?* She held her hand in front of her face and focused her magic through her veins.

The little creases in her hand flashed purple as she focused on the thoughts running through her head. In contemplation, she finally made a fist, pulling everything together and willing her mind into focus. *I can handle this. I won't fail at any of this. I just need to be very calm and strong in my thoughts.* The next morning would welcome her with an unknown sense of adventure. Med had no idea how incredible the coming days would be.

CHAPTER 4

EARLY MORNING

———

The sun shone directly into Med's face like a flashlight. She pulled herself up with a small yawn and a scratch of the head. Her new room was completely different than the one she grew up in; nevertheless, she was excited to get going. She got herself up, brushed her hair, and walked out of her room. Her life was finally exciting. She headed toward the kitchen and passed Shade's room. *I wonder if she's awake.* She decided to knock on the door but got no immediate response.

She heard a moan from inside the room. "Five more minutes," Shade said.

Med left it at that and headed for the kitchen to make some tea. She passed Dixie, who was heading for the shower. Dixie waved.

"Mornin'! Sleep well?" Dixie asked.

"Yeah. As well as you do on your first night anywhere new," Med said.

Dixie smiled and entered the bathroom.

Med took a breath and headed for the living room, where she found Jacks and Scratch watching the early morning news. Scratch seemed infatuated with the way the TV worked while Jacks simply sat with a hand on his chin and a blank expression on his face. Med went to the small kitchen behind them to make some tea.

"You need anything?" Jacks asked.

"I, uh, not really, just looking for tea," she replied. *Why would you phrase it like that?* She inwardly scolded herself.

"Check with Cy. He's outside, and he knows more about this place than I do." Jacks pointed toward the door, keeping an eye on Scratch.

Med walked out of the room to the garage, amazed by the vehicles and the fact that her peers had the craftsmanship and time to make such unique cars. She walked into the bright sun and turned to see Cyset moving steadily. He swayed and moved with a flow. His body wasn't stiff and his eyes were closed. As he moved, he created tornadoes. Small tornadoes, but they were incredibly controlled and precise. He was in a state of focus Med had only seen her mentors achieve.

Med looked on as she saw magic unfamiliar to her. Her eyes held him as he seemingly skated into the air before easing down onto the ground once more.

"Excuse me," Med called, throwing Cyset out of his movement and causing him to fall.

"Oh." He rubbed the back of his head. "Good morning." He popped off the ground. "How you feeling?"

Med stared at him, still trying to put together how he performed that magic.

"Uh, Med?"

"Oh, yeah, it's just, where did you learn that?" she asked. No one had ever let her use that style before.

"You mean where did I learn how to make Wind magic that technical?"

"Yes, especially in that level of ability." She tried to hold in her bewilderment and wonder but couldn't do that without being silent. "I'm not allowed to go that far with my powers at all."

"Well, I mean…" He paused and looked as though he was trying to find the right words. After a moment, he let out a breath. "I've never thought I shouldn't do that with my powers. I've always figured if it can be done with that level of power, then I'll do it."

"You mean, no one's ever put a limit on you or what you can do?" Med asked, trying to wrap her mind around the idea. She tensed up in frustration, thinking about her own experience.

"I've been told what I can't do, just not by other Mages," he said, sighing. "I take it that's what you've been told more than I have?"

Med kept a close eye on him as she tried to see what he was thinking.

What did he mean? He wasn't her, and he didn't know much about her—as far as she knew.

"I've been told a lot of things, yes," she answered.

Cyset raised his hands. "Well, what do you think you can do?"

Med pulled back and stared at him. "Um, y-you know what? I think it won't matter anyway. Can you come inside and help me with the tea kettle?"

Cyset scrunched his face and furled his mouth at the thought but shook his head and followed her inside. Med hoped he wouldn't bring up the conversation again. She looked over to the other part of the room where Scratch and Jacks were still sitting.

"Hey, guys, how's your morning going?" Cyset asked.

"Same as always. Quiet," Jacks said.

"Well, don't get too comfy. We're gonna head to the head-quarters soon for standard evaluation."

Med felt a knot form in her stomach.

"Evaluation?" Her heart began to pound and her mind started racing.

"It's just standard procedure," Cyset said, pushing the button to get the tea ready. "Nothing too major."

Med was terrified and not looking forward to what was coming.

"We'll do it at the new Mystic headquarters they built," he said, handing Med her tea. "It will be simple and quick, I promise."

Med nodded and looked down into the cup. *Okay, simple test, no big deal.* She took a sip of tea. She headed back to her room and found some clothes to wear. As she rummaged through her bag, she found an old purple tracksuit.

Not too flashy and easy to get around in. She pulled on the outfit. Med glanced in the mirror before going back to the living room to find Cyset standing there with a bright yellow jacket and black pants with horizontal yellow stripes.

He turned to see her standing in the doorway. "You ever been to a Mystic headquarters?"

"Once as a kid on a field trip and again to register," Med said.

Med composed herself and waited for the others to show up. Dixie and Shade walked in after a moment. Dixie was wearing a light green plaid shirt with jeans while Shade had a leather jacket and mostly black attire.

"Morning," Shade said, still somewhat groggy.

"Good morning," Med replied.

Jacks and Scratch walked in next. Jacks had a red leather jacket with a black undershirt, blue jeans, and high-top sneakers. Scratch had a bright orange t-shirt with matching shorts and white sneakers.

"Cool, everyone's here. Let's get moving," Cyset said.

Med walked out to the garage and got into Dixie's truck. She looked over to see Jacks and Cyset taking Jacks' red car and looked behind her to see Scratch hop in the back of the truck. She watched Shade get on her motorcycle and they took off. As they drove into Nexi Sciene, they rode through an interwoven pipeline of streets, passing holographic signs and neon boards listing off names and celebrities. Med was hypnotized by the city as she gazed at the world around her. She noticed the team driving up to the Mystic headquarters: forty-seven stories, all meant to help the Mystics of Nexi Sciene. This was the hub of all magic response; the true center of the city. Now it was open to Med and her teammates for the first time.

CHAPTER 5

SHOW AND TELL

———

Med and the rest of the team had traveled to the Mystic headquarters in Nexi Sciene. On floor thirty-four, they stood inside of the new state-of-the-art training center. The floor was whirring up and starting to come online, building up energy and running waves of light. Pillars lifted and fell as it began to calibrate every environment preprogrammed into it. Med stood still looking around, not sure what to do as she waited.

Shade came and tapped her on the shoulder. "So, how you feeling?"

"Good," Med said. "How about you?"

"Oh, you know, tired," Shade said, yawning.

"Did you not sleep well?" Med asked as she saw Shade part her hair.

Shade opened her eyes a little more and chuckled. "No, I slept fine. I'm just not a morning person, that's all."

Med nodded and looked back to Cyset, typing in a sequence on a holographic screen. As he punched in a few more digits, a small rock levitated up into his hands.

"So, where are you from?" Shade asked.

"Soliopolis," Med responded. "You?"

"Nexi Sciene, right in the underbelly," Shade said.

Med lit up. She had never been to Nexi Sciene and had always wanted to go. Before she could ask Shade another question, Cyset clapped his hands and got the attention of the team. He put down a cup and walked over to the common room.

"Alright, let's get down to morning business," Cyset said, holding up a rock. "We need to figure out how much ability we each have, so we're going to use this."

Scratch turned and let out a "Huh?"

"Okay, so," Cyset began. "This rock is considered The Scale. It measures the concentration and focus of a Mage. When you apply your magic to it, it measures your control of your abilities. The more color or the brighter it gets, the higher the control. If you can reflect some properties of your abilities, for example, I make the rock spin in midair like it's in a vortex, that shows extreme control."

"Like a physical?" Dixie asked.

"Pretty much, yes," Cyset said.

Shade piped up, "How do we do that?"

"Simple," said Cyset. "You hold it and focus on it; the same basic stuff we've all done."

Med felt a small shiver go down her spine as she realized what they were going to be doing next. She was always a little nervous during her training before, but she especially didn't like having her teammates as an audience.

"To start off, Jacks, you go first," said Cyset.

Med watched as Jacks walked out into the field, picked up the small sliver of rock, and started focusing his energy on it. Med noticed smoke begin to seep off the rock. It started to glow bright red.

"Whoa," Med whispered.

Jacks stopped and the rock returned to its pure white state. Next, Dixie grabbed the rock and it began to morph and change. It went from a solid to a soil-like substance and returned to its original shape, although light green. The rock levitated off her hand and turned into several forms of sediment. After a moment of focus, Dixie put the rock down.

When it was Shade's turn, she made the rock turn a rich black. The rock's shadow moved out from the ground and levitated parallel to the rock in the air. The shadow gave off the illusion of a three-dimensional image. Shade tossed the rock over to Scratch, who picked it up. At first, nothing happened; after a moment, the group watched the rock turn orange but they also noticed it looked like a small egg. Scratch tossed it to Cyset.

"All right, Med, you're up next," Cyset said.

Med was given the rock. She closed her eyes and imagined the rock by itself and tried to think of what she could do. *How do I show I can heal a rock?* She focused on making the rock return to its most pure state; a clean-cut form free of defects. She opened her eyes to see a purple crystal floating off her hand with no cracks or edges. It was perfectly repaired and pristine. Med dropped the rock and it fell to the ground as she panted heavily.

"Nicely done," said Cyset. "You seem to have a good amount of control over your power."

"What exactly did you think about or do?" Jacks asked.

Med gained some of her breath. "I simply reversed its properties. You know, tried to heal or fix it."

"Interesting," Cyset said.

"So, is that it?" Med asked.

"Not yet," Cyset said. "Now we do a little bit of an exercise."

Med's anxiety returned.

"What are we doing now?" Shade asked.

Cyset pulled a small ball from his pocket and tossed it to Med. She caught it and examined it.

"Should I try manipulating the ball?" she asked.

"Nope, just keep your hands on it," Cyset said. "The rest of us need to keep you off the ground with our abilities."

"Wait, why me?" Med asked.

Cyset turned and said, "So you'll learn to trust us."

Med was confused by what he meant but simply nodded.

"All right, the goal is that flag on the tall pillar over there. Med, head to the green block that signals the start and we'll help you out."

Med kept the ball in her hand and walked to the green block. She took a position while the floor morphed into a marshland. Trees created shadows, the ground was muddy for Dixie, and the flag now sat atop a stone pillar. Med got ready and then heard someone shout "Start!"

She felt the ground shake and the earth below become a floating platform. Other rocks floated up for her to walk on.

"What ya waiting for?" Dixie asked.

Med began hopping from rock to rock. As she leaped, she noticed Scratch hop up, grabbing her with his feet and lifting her over to the next area while flapping his arms.

"Why are you doing that?" she asked.

"If I don't flap my arms, I can't fly like a bird when using that trait," he answered. Scratch pulled her over to the shade and dropped her. The shadows moved around her, carrying her around.

"Ah!" Med squeaked as she slid in a pitch-black wave.

"Don't worry, I've got full control." Shade moved Med through the shadows over to Jacks, who lit fires underneath his feet and grabbed her.

"I have to admit, this is a little scary," Med said.

"You'll get used to it," Jacks said as he carried her above the trees over to the pillars. "All right, I'm gonna throw you and have you walk on air, got it?"

"Wait, what?" Med gasped. "How?"

"Just trust me," Jacks said before tossing Med toward the pillar. As Med's feet swung in the air, she thought she was going to fall until the air beneath her carried her up onto the pillar and dropped her right next to the flag.

Cyset gave her a thumbs up from below. "See, trust exercise. Room deactivate." The room shifted back into the blank void space they had entered as the pillar descended back to the ground and dropped Med off next to Cyset.

"Well, that was interesting," Med said. "You could've told me what you guys were doing."

"It was a *trust* exercise," Cyset said. "Surprise is part of it."

"That's a fun idea," Med joked.

"Fun indeed," said Solaria.

Med looked up to see Solaria in the training room viewing area.

"I'm glad you've all gotten a moment to demonstrate your level of control, but unfortunately, we don't have as much time as we wish," Solaria said.

"What's the issue?" Cyset asked.

"There have been some strange sightings at the Pillars of Rya Drea in the last few days. I thought it best if that was your first task as a group," she said. "I want you to assess what may or may not be happening there. If you can give us a concrete answer, such as an energy surge or simply a lost Mage, we'd appreciate it. Make sure to keep an eye on the town of Mistus in the local area as well."

Med looked at the small rumblings between her friends. Dixie and Shade seemed to be whispering to one another, while Scratch looked excited to get to work. Cyset and Jacks were both silently hopeful. Their faces were smiling with enthusiasm at the idea and looked like they could barely contain the excitement.

"We'll gladly do it," Cyset said.

"Excellent. Good luck with your first task," Solaria said.

Med was nervous. It sounded simple, but nothing was ever easy for her.

CHAPTER 6

FIRST TASK

———

Cyset took in the Pillars of Rya Drea and nodded. He'd always loved coming to see them. Six tall stalactites formed a circle and next to them a view of the sea off the coast of the port city Mistus. The area had been home to multiple Mages and trainers before. He was on guard as he looked at the area, checking for anything suspicious. He felt a chill go up his spine as he looked at a chasm formed around one of the pillars.

"Do you have anything for me, Jacks?" Cyset asked.

Jacks shook his head. "Nah, nothing too abnormal."

Cyset looked at the ground and rubbed his forehead in frustration. *Nothing is out of the ordinary; it's just off. Like the energy in the Pillars has been used by someone else.* He tensed the muscles in his body to keep himself calm while he looked over to Med, who was staring agape at the pillars.

"Wow," she said.

"Pretty cool, right?" Cyset called to get her attention.

He saw Med jerk at the sound of his voice. She turned to him and laughed. "Yeah, this doesn't come close to how mundane Soliopolis was. This is actually something."

"Well, you're standing on some of the earliest structures for magical power. Mages came here for training and early meditation, and it was said that when you came here, your power could increase further if you heard one of the pillars speak," Cyset said, extending his arms.

"Nerd," Shade cried on top of a plateau above Cyset.

He turned to respond but before he could, he heard a howl coming from the chasm. Cyset turned to one of the pillars and stared.

"What was that?" Med asked.

"That's what I want to know myself." Cyset floated over to the chasm and peered down but couldn't make out anything due to its darkness.

The hell? Cyset gazed into the chasm with a heavy heart. His eyes shifted several times looking for crystals that should have been lining the walls and making them glow. He couldn't see the beauty of the chasm or the scriptures that would teach Mages. His mind was racing with possible theories before he was jolted out of his thoughts.

"Hey, Cyset, what's going on?" Scratch yelled from the other side.

Cyset turned in the direction of Scratch's voice to see him standing with Dixie and Jacks.

"Get everyone over here, you need to see this," he cried before turning back toward the gap, looking into the abyss for light and an answer.

"What's up?" Jacks asked.

Cyset turned to his friend and pointed inside the cave. "This cave is supposed to be lit with bright minerals and super diamonds. Instead, it's pitch black."

"Is that cave supposed to be there?" Scratch asked as he looked down over Cyset's shoulder.

The cavity lulled out a moan, and Cyset shook his head. "All right, here's what we do. Jacks, you go ahead of all of us and light the way. Dixie, Shade, you two follow him in there closely. Scratch, you're in the middle, and, Med, hang close to me while I watch our backs."

"You got it, boss," Jacks said, lighting a flame in his palm. Cyset stepped to the side and let his best friend walk in. Dixie crept along behind him.

"This is going to be interesting," Shade quipped.

Med and Scratch walked in, and Cyset followed close behind, making sure to keep an eye on Jacks' flame. He put a hand on the walls to keep himself in the moment.

"Cyset?" Med asked.

"Yeah?" he replied.

"You have any idea what might be down here?" she asked. He looked over to see what she may be thinking and simply shook his head. He didn't voice his assumption.

"I can navigate better with a more active sense. Nose of a dog," Scratch said, activating his magic.

Going farther into the cave, Cyset felt more like he and his team were traveling into some form of an other-worldly portal with purple energy emanating from the walls. They caught his eye and left him bewildered. He hadn't a clue how they had manifested. Cyset looked over at Med, who was moving defensively with her arms wrapped around herself. His gaze shifted back onto what was ahead of him: the image of a person outlined in white kneeling over something.

"Jacks, light up the whole cave!" Cyset yelled as he caught the figure.

Jacks' hand pushed the fire up and created a beam throughout the entire cave. When lit, the cave revealed what the figure was: a person with nearly no muscle on his body;

whatever there was hung from his bones with no definition. Its eyes were hollow and demanding, trying to pry into the souls of the young Mystics.

"What the hell?" Shade said.

Cyset moved to the front of the group next to Jacks, who had his fists clenched and was standing in a defensive posture, ready for a fight.

"Do you mind?" the figure asked.

Cyset and his friends jumped back. He couldn't believe such a low voice came from the figure.

"It talks?" Dixie asked quietly.

"Yeah, apparently," Jacks murmured over his shoulder.

"Who are you?" Cyset asked.

The figure rolled its eyes at him.

The young Mage decided to strengthen his message by making his yellow irises engulf his eyes until they shone goldenly. "I *said*, who are you?"

The figure acknowledged Cyset by looking him up and down. Its entire body moved in jagged directions, cracking and popping with every gesture. Its sunken eyes pierced the air as it gave Cyset the most judgmental look it could.

"So. You're Cyset," the figure said. "How interesting."

Cyset took a step back. "How do you know who I am?"

"That's the price of fame, wouldn't you agree, Jacks?" it said.

Cyset looked over to Jacks, who returned an expression of shock and fear at the figure's statements.

"You two have reputations. The little creature with his senses trained on me does, too, along with shadow girl in the back, the farm girl next to her, and..." It stopped. "And whoever that is."

Cyset looked over his shoulder at the others, all equally shocked. He turned back around and spotted a bag on the ground.

"Why are you in this cave?" Cyset asked. "You may want to come with us for questioning."

"So tempting," the figure said, bowing. "But Solaria is far too powerful at this moment."

"What?" Med and Cyset gasped together.

The figure disappeared and slid into the cave's darkness. The wall then pulled forward and collapsed in on the group. Cyset looked toward Dixie and made a gesture with his hands to signal her.

"Oh, no, ya don't," Dixie said, dropping to the ground and twisting her knuckles into the dirt to stop the walls from falling. The walls stopped, and the cave grew silent as the figure disappeared. "That should do it." She dusted off her hands.

At that moment, the tunnel restructured itself. The walls lost the marble and dense obsidian that had been covering them, and the black dropped off piece by piece to reveal the crystals that covered it before. The crystals lit up the walls and with an aurora of shimmer and gleam.

"What was that? A demon?" Shade asked, her voice shaking.

"No, I've seen demons. They don't do that," Scratch said.

"It had to be a Mage!" Jacks exclaimed.

"He could've been a Shadow User. If you focus hard enough, you can control the light of certain areas," Shade added.

"What kind of Shadow User does this?" Dixie asked.

"We'll get our answer with that," Cyset said, pointing to the bag on the floor. "There may be something in it that gives us something."

He grabbed the bag and began looking into it for anything he could find and pulled out a small mineral. The rock wasn't processed and was pulsing with energy. It looked corrupted because of how black it was.

"What is that?" Med asked.

"I believe this is our first piece of evidence," Cyset said, showing her the rock.

She was instantly entranced.

"Med," Shade called, snapping her fingers in Med's face.

Med jolted back to reality and shook her head.

"All right, so that's evidence. What's the play now, boss?" Jacks asked.

"We get to work looking for our culprit. We'll search Mistus, and if we find anyone or anything with information, we get moving," Cyset said.

"That's the best we can do?" Jacks asked.

"For now," Cyset said. "The more we know the better." He motioned his team to head back up the cave to the outside. He looked at the rock and gripped it tight in his hands. *What the hell is going on right now?* As he began walking, something grabbed his arm.

"Cyset?" Med asked.

He turned to see her peering over his shoulder. She was taking another look at the rock.

"What in the world is going on right now?" Med asked.

Cyset took a breath and blinked for a moment before answering.

"I don't have a good answer for you," Cyset said, urging her to follow. All he knew was there needed to be an answer and the closest place to look for now was Mistus.

CHAPTER 7

INVESTIGATION

For Med, the smell of the sea was familiar, but the town and bustling port wasn't. She had never been to Mistus and stayed as close to Shade as she could while walking along the port. She was astonished by the large crowd of people she was trapped in. Everything she saw was making her gasp in awe.

"Med," Shade called to her.

Med turned, and Shade waved her on.

"Stay close. I don't think I'll be able to find you if I lose you in the crowd," Shade said.

"Sorry, I'm just a little blown away—" Med said before bumping into a drunk man.

"Hey, watch it!" the drunk snapped.

"Sorry," Med said. She saw him look her up and down and scowl at her.

Shade jumped in front of Med, blocking the man. "She said sorry, now piss off," Shade barked.

The drunk left them alone and staggered along.

"Are you all right?" a passing sailor asked. He was burly and older than them by a fair margin. He looked like he had just gotten done with a long shift on the docks but seemed jolly.

"Oh, I'm fine. I just wasn't paying attention," Med said.

"Seemed like he wasn't either. You looking for something?" the older man asked.

"We are looking for someone," Shade said.

"Oh, really?" He folded his arms.

"Have you seen someone suspicious around for these last few days? A very slender, bony man with sunken eyes?" Med asked.

"Can't say that I have. Why? You two Mystics?" he asked.

"Yes, that's why we need to know," Shade said.

"Well, I'll keep my eye out," the man said.

"Okay, take care," Med said, walking away.

"Happy hunting," the man told her and Shade as they continued.

Med looked to Shade, shaking her head in frustration. Med understood; they had been looking for information for a few hours now and had found nothing.

"So, do you think being a Mystic is rewarding?" Med asked, trying to ease the tension of searching for their mysterious figure.

Shade sighed. "Well, it's pretty quaint here—not like Nexi Sciene." Shade adjusted her hair.

The two walked over to a stand where Dixie and Scratch were waiting.

"How'd it go for you two?" Med asked.

"Not well. We couldn't get any info about anything," Dixie said. "Did get a good view of the sites around this port, though, and met a nice lady with a flower stand down the street."

"There was no scent in the cave for me to track him, and no animals mentioned a skeleton with thin skin walking around," Scratch said.

"You talk to animals?" Shade asked.

"How do you think I learned to speak and have basic conversation?" Scratch asked.

Med raised a finger but then immediately dropped it as she felt the answer unnecessary.

"Same here," Cyset said, walking up from behind. "Nothing."

Med turned her attention to Jacks, who seemed annoyed. "Are you okay?"

Jacks blew out some air before answering. "I'm not a coast city guy."

"What, don't like seafood?" Shade asked.

"I don't mind seafood. I just don't like where it comes from," Jacks said.

"Why wouldn't you like water?" Scratch asked.

"You being serious right now?" Jacks asked. "I'm a Fire Rat. I can't create fire submerged in water. Not to mention the whole port next to me could extinguish my flames."

Med watched Cyset grab Jacks' shoulder and remind him to calm down.

"Let's just try and figure out what's up with our whole mysterious cave figure, please," Cyset said, rubbing his brow.

Med looked over the port and spotted a souvenir shop nearby selling diamonds. While the rock they found was unknown, she figured they probably had something to add.

"Hey, why don't we try there?" She pointed to the shop.

"That souvenir place?" Cyset asked.

"Yeah. It could have something about local minerals and give us some information," Med said.

"Hey, it's something," Shade added, shrugging her shoulders.

Med looked to Cyset, who nodded and walked over to the shop. She followed him inside. The store was aglow with diamonds and decorative items aplenty. On a shelf were decorated heads and necklaces, on another snow globes and mini boats to take home.

"Good morning, you two. Anything I can help you with?" a clerk asked.

Med walked over to the counter with Cyset.

"We're Mystics, and we need to know what this rock is," Cyset said, putting it on the counter.

The clerk examined the rock closely. "It's been distorted, but it's used to encase someone's magic if need be."

"Encase magic?" Med asked.

"Hold on, what?" Shade asked.

"It's probably a Sorcerer Sulfate," Dixie said.

Med turned to Dixie. The other Mystics did too.

"What?" Dixie asked. "Just because I grew up in a place where not a lot of people use magic doesn't mean I don't know about sediments."

"Okay, but what else would we know?" Cyset asked.

Med turned to the clerk, still examining the rock and pushing it down.

The clerk shrugged his shoulders and looked at the Mystics with a disgruntled face. "As far as I can tell, the last we heard was that only Dark Angels could put magic into rocks like this."

Med felt her heart jump as she looked up at the clerk and began to sweat profusely. "What?"

"Oh, yes, it's an old myth. A Dark Angel could infuse their powers into a rock and begin to haunt people with their energy."

"What do you mean a myth?" Med asked.

"It's a story that says when a Dark Angel learns about this power, they begin to abuse it," the clerk said. "They transform into some sort of monster and begin to hurt themselves."

"No, they don't!" Med exclaimed.

"How would you know?"

"Because *I* can't do that!" Med stormed out the door into an alleyway to regain herself. She hadn't heard this before, and it was terrifying. She felt her heart pounding out of her chest and thought she might throw up at the thought.

Dark Angels can do that? Why didn't anybody tell me?

She screamed silently until she felt a hand on her left shoulder. She turned to see Shade and Dixie standing over her.

"Hey, whoa, look at me, look at me," Shade said calmly. "Just look at me, all right?"

Med began to let out gasps of air.

"Okay, you good?" Shade asked.

"Yes," Med gasped. "Yeah, yeah, I'm all right."

"Good, just stay with us," Shade said.

Both Dixie and Shade stared directly at Med as she pulled herself together. After a moment, she walked with them out of the alleyway toward where Cyset, Jacks, and Scratch were standing.

"You okay?" Jacks asked.

"Oh, yeah. I'm just a little off-tilt," Med said. "I felt a little sick from something earlier."

"Well, don't worry about it. The clerk gave us a bit more information on the myth after we brought Scratch a skull. He basically haggled us into purchasing something," Cyset said.

"Okay, now what?" Scratch asked, clenching said skull in hand.

"Take the rock back and examine it. Nothing else we can do," Cyset said.

Med was quietly panting while the group walked through Mistus. Everything was still spinning but she tried not to show it so her teammates wouldn't hound her with questions. Her mind was a swirling wave of thoughts that plagued her throughout the day. She didn't know how Dark Angels could infuse their magic into objects. What was terrifying her was the question of why wasn't she told?

CHAPTER 8

MEET ARGUS

———

Cyset sat at an examination desk in the complex with documents staring him in the face. The room was used for investigation and observation and behind the desk was a clipboard and map of Mystian with every location mapped out. He read through a list of all known magic compounds and documented energies, looking for a solution to what he had seen in the cave; he wasn't going to allow himself to accept no as an answer.

The documents had come from everyone and everywhere, and none of them were giving him something he could use. His head pulsed as he racked his brain over the information like he was trying to smash through a brick wall with his skull. *I have a theory, but it isn't extremely possible—there are not enough of them around anywhere.* The detective monologue plaguing his head was interrupted by the sound of footsteps. He turned his head to see Med coming into the room.

"Afternoon," he said. "You need anything?"

Med glided through the room, seemingly still possessed by a ghost. She walked around without looking at him; she was only focused on the rock and the energy inside of it.

"Med," Cyset tried again.

He still got no answer.

"Med!" he yelled.

Med jumped. Now she finally opened her mouth.

"I just—" Med paused and took a breath before finishing. "I just had a bit of a flash earlier, because of what that guy said."

Cyset sat up as he asked, "Flash?"

"It's just shocking, you know, hearing about your powers like that," Med said.

Cyset raised an eyebrow and resumed working on the rock. He felt like she wasn't telling him everything, but before Cyset could do anything else, one of the documents began to flip about in front of him. It got up and started walking as if possessed. His eyes followed the papers and he looked over to Med. "That's not you, right?"

"No."

Next, the walls began to shrink and blur as if they were an oil painting moving around them. The room filled with black, and the walls became pure voids. Nothing could be seen on them, and no light could reflect off them.

"Guys, I need you in here now!" Cyset called.

The other Mages came running in just as the world around them became some sort of alternate vision of everything they had seen.

The floor became a pond of tar beneath them, yet they didn't sink. Cyset's yellow eyes focused on the floor before he peered up and saw the same skeleton figure from the cave. He felt the muscles in his body tighten with anticipation as he stared it dead in its eyes. It snapped its bones and began contorting and popping itself in and out of place. It stared back at him then turned to look around at the group.

"Mmm, that was a trip," the thing said as it moved directly in front of Cyset.

Cyset stayed as still as he could. It reminded him of one of the caricatures he would train against when he was younger. "How the hell are you here?" he asked through gritted teeth.

"Don't worry about it," it said. "Worry about yourselves, since none of you seem very tough."

"Oh, is that what you think?" Jacks asked. "Coming from a skinny, dying remnant of a being itself."

"Itself?" it snarled, twisting its neck sideways.

"Well, who the hell are you if you're a person?" Shade asked.

The figure sighed with incredible disdain. "I am Argus."

Cyset stiffened. Argus was the name of one of the oldest Mages in history, said to have been around a few centuries before Cyset was born; a Mage who worked to destroy everything Solaria built and ruin the compromise between all Mages and Non-Mages. The most important thing about him was his Mage type. Dark Angel.

"So, you're the famed magic terrorist?" Cyset said. "What an honor."

Argus twisted his head to scare him. "Oh, listen to you. The lost Wind Wizard, born at sunset with no mother at sunrise," Argus mocked.

Cyset made a fist.

"What do you want?" Jacks asked.

Argus twisted his head on his body to look at Jacks. "I would like to be rich, and yet here I sit, powerless. I want to have my power back, but I've lived far too long. I would love nothing more than to be able to speak and enlighten others to the treasure I believe they should possess."

"What exactly does that mean?" Cyset questioned.

"Keep grinding your teeth, boy. It will probably do you some good." Argus's gaze shifted to Med. "Now then, who— or *what*—are you?"

Med folded her arms at the statement. "I'm a Mage, and unlike you, I heal people instead of killing them."

Cyset smiled at Med's defiance.

"Heal, is that all you can do?" Argus said. "So if I hurt one of your friends, will you fix their pain?"

"Oh, please try, I'd love to see if you can fight looking like that," Shade said.

"Really? Well then." Argus began moving his arms and causing his entire body to line up with a purple aura before he flung the table and paper at the Mystics. "Observe." Each item flew around them like a pack of locusts.

Cyset quickly used the wind underneath him to flip around and dodge every object.

"Shell of a turtle," Scratch said, hardening his body to repel anything that hit him.

Jacks lit up his hands and began flinging fire at the random pieces of paper flying at his face.

Shade looked over at Argus and spoke "Shadow Control" in reverse.

Argus's body was held still by the shadow coming off the light of his aura.

Cyset turned to Med, who touched the table and caused one of the legs to revert to its original state. The room turned back to normal in an instant with the others trying to figure out what was going on.

Argus showed genuine astonishment for the first time. "So, Solaria's infected your mind, fellow Dark Angel?"

"Fellow?" Med asked.

"Yes," Argus said.

Now Cyset pushed Argus up against the wall with the wind holding him in place. In a fit of frustration, he held

Argus down. "Not like you'll get to revel in it, Argus. Now turn yourself in."

Argus sneered at Cyset before melting into the wall and sliding away as a puddle.

"What the—how did he do that?" Shade yelled, freaked out.

"He's a Dark Angel, so he most likely manipulated his energy to shift his autonomy and body," Med said.

"Dark Angels can do that?" Dixie asked, confused.

"I've never been sure before," Med said. "I don't know if I can do that."

"Well, where is he?" Jacks asked.

"I don't know. I don't have his scent anywhere around us," Scratch said.

"Oh, believe me, I'm everywhere, children." Argus's voice echoed through the walls, encompassing the Mystics. "I've got quite the fun little game of hide and seek planned for you."

"I don't like playing stupid games," Cyset said. His eyes searched for Argus's new shape.

"Oh, but here's the thing: I didn't know about my fellow Mage until I saw her," Argus said. Cyset's eyes widened as he realized how Argus learned about them. "No news reports, interviews, podcast bits, nothing—almost as if having a Dark Angel wandering around could be an issue for you…"

"That's not good," Scratch said.

"Oh, no, Scratch, it isn't," Argus snarked.

"What happens when you reveal yourself and Solaria sends as many Mystics as she can after you?" Shade asked.

"I set off the rock," Argus answered.

"The rock?" Cyset asked. After doing so he noticed the rock from earlier was gone. He inferred that Argus had swiped it from the desk. *Son of a bitch.*

"Putting it simply, this rock is infused with my energy and once I set it off, it'll infect all of Nexi Sciene, giving me control of the city's energy and ability to bend it to my imagination. Maybe manipulate a few blocks, cause something to walk that shouldn't, or hurt someone who needs it," Argus said.

Cyset's mind went into overdrive with the possibilities. The last few moments led him to believe anything could happen and he may have to accept Argus wasn't bluffing.

"You'll have to find me and the rock. Good luck little Mages." Argus's voice faded into the air.

Cyset immediately banged his fist on the wall out of frustration. *Damn it, I didn't need this today.* His mind was ahead of his body. He put together what he was going to say before turning around to the others. "There's a chance he's lying, but we're not in a situation to take risks."

"You got a plan?" Jacks asked.

"As much of a plan as I can come up with," Cyset said, nodding. "We split up and cover as much ground as we can. If we find either Argus or the rock, get them. Shade, Jacks, and I are going to check the lower areas of Nexi Sciene. Shade knows them, and we can navigate easier. Med, Dixie, Scratch, you go through the upper levels in the Tech District. It'll be less of a maze. As soon as you find the rock, take it to the Mystics' Operations Center in the middle of the city. If you find Argus, try to stall him until we all get there."

"Right, got it," Dixie said.

Cyset felt like he had a plan for himself but every bit of the situation felt like a Hail Mary attempt. He couldn't guarantee he would get Argus; all he could guarantee was that they weren't going down without a fight.

He and his group headed to the garage and hopped into Jacks' car. Dixie let Scratch and Med jump into her truck, and the group drove into the brightly lit and colorful techno sanctuary known as Nexi Sciene. Cyset knew the team had to either find Argus or let him get his hands on a vast playground of super tech.

CHAPTER 9

PRODIGIES

———

In Nexi Sciene, below the neon lights, was an underground of dark streets filled with people. Multiple individuals wandered around and found refuge there. The top of the city didn't give them a home, so they were forced to make one in the dark slums. Cyset had his hands full with his teammates as they walked past the trash and gutters looking for any sign or trace of Argus. The neighborhood crawled with unsuspecting people. He couldn't picture a way to draw Argus out from where he was hiding without startling the crowds.

He scanned his surroundings as he walked across the street and began to find his way through the dark. There were no bright lights or beautiful colors; it was dull and bleak as they trudged through the gray. Cyset lost focus on what was in front of him and bumped into a person on the street.

"Whoa, sorry," Cyset said.

The man turned with saliva flowing from his mouth, disoriented and drunk. "You little freak, watch it," he slurred, lumbering out into the street.

Jacks watched the man stagger past them with Shade putting her hands on her hips and shaking her head.

"Doesn't seem like there is a lot of hope down here," Jacks asked.

"They don't really have a lot to hope for," Shade said. "This isn't a huge neon light area; it's the slums. You learn to be tough and how to fight down here."

Cyset felt his stomach drop. He had always had someone to rely on, and now he was seeing just how little that prepared him for this experience. He never lived in the slums, nor did he really know much about them. *I've got the map of this place memorized—just not the atmosphere.*

"I guess that's not something I'm used to," Cyset said to Shade.

Jacks patted him on the shoulder. "That's not your fault man. Neither am I. All we gotta do is find Argus, and we'll have done our part for today." Jacks walked over to the corner of the street, and Cyset followed.

The group continued farther into the dark streets, past homeless people, broken glass bottles, and brick walls as opposed to palladium steel. Now farther into the city's underbelly, they stumbled upon an avenue of apartments. These buildings were not as dark as the others and seemed to have some level of color to them.

"The hell are these?" Cyset asked. He hadn't seen these before and didn't think they'd exist. The neighborhood had always been considered undesirable growing up.

"Those were being added a while back. Apparently, they're new residences for people moving into the neighborhood," Shade said.

Jacks shook his head at the idea. "People are just moving here now?"

"Hey, I grew up in the chapel, so I didn't get the full experience. I knew about the ins and outs and what would happen, but I was never in the crossfire. I had a chance and some hope in my upbringing," Shade said.

"Excuse me," a voice said.

Cyset turned to a woman staring them down.

She walked down the steps of her apartment and cried out, "Who are you kids?"

"I swear," Shade said through gritted teeth. "If one more person calls us kids or children today..."

Jacks signaled to hold her back. Cyset simply put his hands up to show there was nothing in them and looked at the woman with a calm expression. He knew to speak slowly.

"Don't worry, ma'am," he said, walking over. "We're just Mystics doing a small investigation."

"Well, I don't think there are any Mages here, so you need to go," the woman said.

"I'm afraid that's not possible at the moment. We still need to search a few blocks. Don't worry, it's a small situation," Cyset said.

"No, you need to leave, and you shouldn't be here in this neighborhood. There are no Mages here and there shouldn't be," she said.

Cyset looked back at Jacks and Shade who simply shrugged their shoulders.

"I don't follow," Cyset said, turning back around.

"There are no Mages in this neighborhood, and we don't need any."

"We still have jurisdiction to investigate this area and look around for any possible suspects," Cyset said.

"Listen, either you and your friends leave or I'll be forced to call the police." The woman pulled out her phone.

"I understand. Have a nice day," Cyset said, walking back to the other two. "That's gonna be an issue," he whispered under his breath. He walked past Shade and Jacks and gestured for them to keep up.

Jacks matched his stride. "What was that about?"

"Just keep walking and leave her be," Cyset said, holding back his frustration.

They headed farther down and came upon a strip with a couple of restaurants. He looked over to his exhausted friends and decided they should stop at the pizzeria. He sat on the curb out front and took a moment to think about what they would do next, considering they hadn't found Argus.

"God, I hate this," Shade said. "That little skeleton is probably laughing at us right now from wherever he is."

Cyset sighed at the thought.

"Maybe he was actually bluffing about his whole plan and just did this to create a red herring," Jacks noted. "He could probably be several miles away from Nexi Sciene by now."

Cyset rubbed his forehead and looked up at the city's skyline. He tried to gather his thoughts around what may or may not be happening with Argus until he heard something—a siren.

He looked over his shoulder at a police car turning the corner and parking on the sidewalk behind him. He thought the car was just parking to get a perfect spot until he heard the officer cry out.

"You three," the officer said.

"Shit," Jacks and Cyset said together.

The officer dialed in on his radio about the group while Jacks and Cyset slowly raised their hands.

"The hell are you two doing?" Shade asked.

"Being careful," Cyset said.

"Most cops are Non-Mages. I can easily trip him up," Shade whispered.

"Don't. Just put your hands up and don't do anything crazy," Jacks said.

Shade put up her hands while looking at the officer.

"All of you, don't move!" the officer yelled.

"He's scared; he won't see it coming," Shade urged.

"That's the problem." Cyset turned slowly while speaking to the officer. "I'm unarmed, and I have no magic activated. I'm showing you my hands." He faced the officer and saw his hand close to a weapon. Gun or not, he didn't want to do anything to set the officer off.

"I've got a call about you. Two tall dark-skinned kids, one with yellow eyes, and a small pale one. Said you were causing a disturbance. What are you doing here?"

"We're Mystics. Just allow me to pull my ID out, and I'll show you."

"I said, don't move!" This time, the officer yelled and shook his fist at Cyset before grabbing his weapon.

"He's terrified," Shade whispered to Jacks.

"No shit," Jacks returned.

Cyset shushed both of them and kept his eyes on the officer.

"You're all coming with me, you understand?" the officer said.

"Okay, okay," Cyset said.

"What do we do about Argus?" Shade asked.

"I don't know. Just follow our lead if you don't wanna get shot," Jacks said.

Cyset felt his heart beating out of his chest. He had a weapon ready to fire on him, Jacks, and Shade, and he also had a rogue Mage running around. It felt like the world was closing in, hoping to pull him into the dirt.

CHAPTER 10

OUTLANDERS

———

In the Business District, Med stayed close to Dixie, hoping to keep an idea of where to go and what was going on. People moved about as men and women in suits trudged along the sidewalks. By now, the sun had set and neon lights illuminated the streets. Billboards played the products all around them and the colors reflected off the sides of buildings. Med did her best to keep an eye on Scratch and Dixie; she didn't want to get lost in Nexi Sciene with no way of navigating through it. Thankfully, Scratch's orange outfit made him stand out in a crowd.

"Scratch, wait up!" Med called, looking past Dixie. "We need to stay together."

Scratch was a bit far off but he paused. "Sorry, sorry," Scratch said, panting and gasping. "It's all so huge and cool and bright." His eyes were lit with wonder, and Med envied his ability to get used to this situation so quickly while she was trying her best to focus on the task at hand.

"Well, for the time being," Dixie said, looking at both of them, "stay close to me and don't go too far away."

Med felt a wave of relief come over her thanks to Dixie being able to control and understand what was happening around them. Her thoughts could correct around Dixie.

"Right, no problem," Scratch said.

"Yes," Med said, nodding.

Med continued down the district with her friends and looked for anything out of the ordinary. She caught Dixie looking over at her.

"You all right over there?" Dixie asked.

Med didn't want to be awkward and quickly replied, "Oh, I'm fine."

"Don't worry, it's not an interrogation. I just want to make sure you don't get caught up staring at lights." Dixie put a hand on Med's shoulder. "You'll learn how to get used to the city life if you stay around enough."

"You... uh, right." Med thought of something. "So, what were you before being a Mystic?"

"Farmgirl. I had to learn about being careful from experience. I'm actually glad I'm not alone in that fact." Dixie smiled.

Med looked down and then back at Dixie. "I guess I haven't been thinking like that."

"Well, you can at least rest assured that the sky won't fall if you step wrong. Relax a little."

Med was about to reply but they were interrupted.

"Hey, I found something," Scratch said, sniffing. He held his nose with a moan. "Something terrible."

Med noticed he was standing over a grate above the sewage system. "Oh, Scratch, that's because you are smelling a sewer."

"Why does that exist?" Scratch asked, still holding his nose.

Dixie and Med started chuckling, and Med then felt a chill run down her body. It felt like an alarm bell.

"Med?" Dixie asked.

"I-I feel something… some sort of power. Like the feeling I get when I activate my abilities." Med held her heart. "I think I can use it to find the rock, if it is infused with Argus's energy."

"How you figure that?" Scratch asked.

"I believe it's a talent I have due to being a Dark Angel. I can sense and feel energy to help convert it."

"Which way then?" Scratch asked, hopping up next to them.

Med closed her eyes and tried to control her energy around the tingle. Her whole body activated as if every nerve and bone had a new overload of senses to them. She opened her eyes and saw a trail of magic, an aura leading to a line of buildings across the street.

"Over there," Med said, pointing. "It feels like it's at its strongest over there around those apartments."

The group crossed the street amidst some very high traffic and walked into an alley. It was dark, only lit up with the moonlight around it. Med could see the aura permeating from the ground at the end of the alley with more energy than anything close to it. The three inched their way to the new rock on the ground. Med was in front of her friends and had her sights focused on the rock.

She got closer and kneeled over it. It was shuffled between trash bags and scum. It radiated energy and was causing the bricks behind it to crack. Med didn't want to touch the rock without a precaution, so she moved her hand closer and felt the tingle grow to an itch. Her aura was welling up around her arm, and she began to get the chills. As her hand touched the rock, the object vanished. The energy pulled away from her and went up into the air like a puff of smoke.

"What'd you do?" Dixie asked.

"I didn't do anything. I just tried to touch it!" Med screeched.

"Well, then where did it go?" Scratch asked.

"The better question would be, did it ever exist?" Med turned around to see Argus standing at the opposite end of the alleyway with his hands behind his back.

"Hello again," he said.

"Holy hell," Dixie said.

Med deadlocked her eyes on Argus as she was trying to put together how he got there so quickly. She saw him twisting his head sideways and smiling as though the body he was in was possessed by the devil. Med felt a chill again run down her body as she stared at the other Dark Angel.

"Well, what now?" Scratch asked.

Argus chuckled before lifting his fingers and causing the alleyway entrance behind him to be blocked by pitch-black emptiness. The sky above morphed into a crimson red and the moon in the sky a black circle. The haze left them embedded into a world that seemed to mark the end rather than the future.

"Now, I show you the power you have never fully seen," Argus said, straightening.

CHAPTER 11

THE POWER OF A DARK ANGEL

In a now-closed alley, amidst the Business District of Nexi Sciene, Argus the Dark Angel stood before Med and her friends, who were unsure of what to do next. While she'd been trained to defend herself and how to fight, Med had never actually done it. She'd never expected to duel somebody. Her body stiffened, and she held her breath in the face of a Dark Angel who was set on performing domestic terrorism. She didn't know what was about to happen, and she didn't want to find out either; however, this wasn't a battle that could be avoided.

Argus's body moved like watercolors dripping down a canvas. His body slithered in all directions like a snake. He looked like he was getting ready to enjoy harming the Mystics while also pushing their minds to the breaking point. Med looked to Dixie and saw the face of someone who didn't fear their enemy. She looked to Scratch and saw a predator ready to pounce. *I need to become the Mage I think I can be for this struggle if I want to make it out.* Of course, this was easier to think than do, especially right now.

The power welling inside of Med began to feel uncontrollable. She saw Argus's body begin to swell as the magic made his veins glow purple and an aura outlined his figure. It was incredibly visible, to the point she felt as though she could touch it. She shivered and her mind raced.

"Ah, hell," Dixie said, putting her hands up in front of her face to brace for the fight.

"Claws out!" Scratch said, summoning the power of a tiger's claws to his hands and lowering his body into the stance of an animal ready to pounce.

Med swallowed hard and blinked. She stared at Argus, merely a silhouette due to the magic overshadowing his body. He twitched as he moved his hands toward the sky and the power emanating from him floated over to a fire escape.

"The first thing you shall witness," Argus said, "is how much more interesting I can make the world." The fire escape moved and began to slither and slide down the building toward them. Med gasped and was on the ground before she realized Dixie had tackled her out of the way.

"You good?" Dixie asked.

"Yeah, thanks," she said as she looked to see Scratch bounce off the wall and head directly for Argus's face, only to fly right back at them into a dumpster.

"Trash, once and always." Argus laughed as he flung Scratch through the air.

Dixie then jumped up and began throwing small pebbles from her pockets at Argus. They were caught in mid-air by Argus's energy and held in place.

"Is that how you plan to beat me, with minor pebbles?" he asked brashly.

"Not quite," Dixie said as she made her mark glow. "Expand!" The rocks then grew, covering Argus in soot and holding him to the ground.

"Damn it!" Argus cried.

Med took her chance and tried to make something attack Argus. She was able to make a piece of plastic on the ground go after Argus; sadly, it did nothing but bounce off of him.

"Are you kidding me?" Argus asked.

Med began to breathe heavily from the anxiety of helplessness.

"Cover your ears," Scratch called from behind them. The two did as he instructed as Scratch yelled like a rabid canary, shaking Argus. Argus winced at the sound and then made the electric cable running up the building wrap around Scratch's mouth.

"Silence is golden, don't you know?" Argus said as he caused the ground holding Scratch in place to explode from underneath him. He stalked forward toward the three of them.

Argus stepped closer, his energy radiating. "Now I'll show you how to hit hard." His energy pulsed into his fist and shot out like a lightning bolt.

Med barely dodged the blast as it scraped her shoulder, leaving behind a gash. She winced as she moved out of the way. Argus then tried again, this time aiming directly at Dixie's head. This shot narrowly missed as Dixie ducked and came around, hitting Argus square on the chin.

Argus's head popped up like a toy robot as he reeled back, only to feel the force of Scratch leaping over Dixie and kicking him like a kangaroo. As Argus wobbled backward, Med moved out of instinct. She managed to kick Argus hard in the stomach, knocking him to the ground. Her heart beat out of her chest as he fell.

"I think you forgot you're a little stick bug there, didn't ya?" Scratch joked.

Med could see Argus trying to recover. As he got up slowly, he didn't heal himself. He stood up, holding his midsection, and didn't use any energy to heal; he was simply fighting on his own power.

"What the...?" Med whispered to herself. "Why isn't he trying to heal himself?"

Argus coughed, and he tried to regain his breath.

"I'd say you should stop while you're ahead, old skelebrator," Dixie said.

Argus spit out blood in their direction

Med felt her stomach drop, fearing the worst was yet to come as she saw Argus smile.

"Not yet," he said. The spit began to morph. It constructed into an outline of a person, standing straight up. It was nothing more than a silhouette built out of ooze. It jumped over the heads of the Mystics, amazing them with its speed. It landed behind them and now had them cornered.

Med looked over to Dixie and frantically asked, "What do I do? I don't know how to fight that!" She stayed close in the hopes her friend could keep her covered.

"Just grit your teeth and think of someone or something you don't like," Dixie said.

The silhouette charged forward, spinning like a tornado. Scratch ducked while Dixie pulled Med away from it. The silhouette jumped toward Dixie and Med, missing them at first and then jumping off the wall and pouncing toward Scratch. The silhouette landed in front of him and swung at his head. The Animal Magician ducked again and rolled under the silhouette's legs. It came around and went for his head, only to have Scratch grab its arm.

Scratch jumped up and flipped the silhouette on its back only to immediately hop up and spin again, this time in the direction of Dixie. She pushed Med away and put her fists in front of her face, ducking and swaying and trying to dodge the crazy flailing arms of the silhouette. It was wild and unhinged. It had no direction. It was just madly swinging, looking to inflict as much damage as it could. It kept going until Dixie began swinging at its body, causing it to crumble and turn to smoke.

The smoke then grabbed Dixie and pulled her down. It had a lock around her neck and the smoke began to squeeze as she fought to pull it off. Med was frozen, unable to move from her position as she watched her friend fight the smoke.

"Hey, back off!" Scratch said as he grabbed for the smoke. It instantly infiltrated his nostrils, causing him to cough as he reeled back. "That *smell*! The sewer is back!" He gasped, collapsing to his knees.

Med shook in fear and hurt as she watched. She turned her head to see Argus laughing. Her fear turned to anger and her blood boiled—she was staring at the cause of all her problems.

The thoughts that ran through her head kept reminding her how Dark Angels were feared and hated. The flood of rage overwhelmed her, and Argus was no longer a person or just a Mage to her; he was a target in the alleyway and the only thing putting him in view was a haze of red. She made a fist and felt anger overtake her. She lifted her hand and put her palm to a dumpster. The dumpster moved before jumping over to Argus and punching him straight in the face with its bulk. He was sent flying and hit the dark wall on the other end.

The hit he took caused his focus to finally falter and the smoke dissipated. Dixie and Scratch regained their breath, and Med pulled objects from the area together. She grabbed trash cans, discarded paper, metal, and sheets of plastic as she turned it into a cobbled-together Titan. It stared Argus down and made a move to stop him.

"Med, no!" Dixie yelled.

This snapped Med out of her rage. She turned to see her friends okay and beginning to get up. She ran over to help them as fast as she could. "Scratch, Dixie, are you two all right?"

"Yes," Dixie said.

"I think so, at least I don't have to deal with that smell anymore," Scratch said.

Med let out a sigh of relief before she realized Argus was still over on the other side of the alleyway. He was still sitting against the wall with a small stream of blood coming from his mouth. His grin remained, however, as he looked over at the Mystics before he raised his hands again.

"What now?" Dixie asked.

"Don't worry, we'll meet again," Argus said as he began to sink into the ground. "Well done, little sister, you've taken a big first step." His voice echoed as he disappeared. With that, the world reverted to its original state and became a normal environment once more.

"Wha-what did he just—?" Dixie stammered.

Med sank to her knees, looking at her hands in disbelief. The Titan collapsed with her as the junk fell and began to roll around. Med panted heavily as she started to feel the weight of what she had just done. Then she felt Dixie's hand touch her shoulder. "Hey, hey, what happened? What's going on?"

Med didn't look at her; she just put her hands down. "We need to get to the Mystics' Operations Center. Now."

CHAPTER 12

CLAIMS AND CONFUSION

———

Med sat in an office with Dixie and Scratch, her eyes focused on the floor. She couldn't let go of what Argus said as he disappeared.

"Well done, little sister" played in her head over and over as she grasped her ears, hoping the echoes would fade out. Dixie had a hand on her shoulder. She felt like she was staring into a void as she sat there. She couldn't bear to meet her teammate's gaze as she thought about what had happened in that leeway. She couldn't bring herself to speak or move.

"He was trying to mess with you," said Dixie. "You didn't do anything close to what he did. It was simply an adrenaline rush overwhelming you."

Med didn't react to Dixie's words. She simply kept her eyes focused down. She was about to fall back into her thought process as the door opened in the room. She immediately snapped out of it at the sight of Solaria.

She started shaking because she couldn't begin to think of how Solaria would react. Did she know Med used her magic beyond her training? Was she angry?

Questions bounced in her head until Solaria said, "Oh, thank goodness! All of you are okay."

Med sighed in relief. *She's just checking on us.* "

I had to go clear up an issue involving your team-mates already."

Med looked over to see Cyset standing at Solaria's shoulder.

"What happened?" Dixie asked, concerned.

Cyset scratched the back of his head and groaned. "Let's just say someone made a miscalculation," he said before opening his yellow eyes wide. "More importantly, what the heck happened with you guys? I was told you came in here and reported that you saw Argus and then got into a fight with him?"

Scratch jumped over Med and Dixie and popped up in front of Cyset. "Oh, my gosh, dude, it was nuts! Argus did this thing where he made the sky turn red and then he blocked off the alleyway and started flying at us, and I flew into a dumpster and Dixie punched him. I kicked him and Med kicked him too and then a silhouette came after us and then Dixie and I got strangled and then Med did something I don't remember and then he left."

Med looked at a blank-faced Cyset.

"I got enough of that, I think," Cyset said, processing the information. "But hey, nice job kicking Argus, man. High five." He raised his hand, which Scratch pounced up to hit.

Jacks and Shade walked into the room, glancing at the other three with a look of concern.

Shade walked over to Med and Dixie and kneeled near the two of them. "You two all right?"

"Shaken, but mostly okay," Dixie said.

"I believe so," Med said.

Shade looked her directly in the eyes.

"Where were you guys?" Scratch asked.

Jacks folded his arms and scoffed at the question. "Simply put, dealing with unfriendly Non-Mages." He leaned against the wall.

"A woman got upset with us being in her neighborhood and decided to call the authorities. You know, the ones who are not Mystics," Cyset explained.

"I believe now that you're all here, I should inform you of my next action," Solaria said.

"What's that?" Dixie asked.

"With the return of Argus to the current world, I believe we now have a bit more of an issue on our hands. As much as I want to leave Argus to Mystic jurisdiction, unless we can offer a permanent solution, other entities will try to take control."

"This is why I hate bureaucracy," Cyset said.

"Despite personal opinions," Solaria said, raising her brow at Cyset, "this is a time to be incredibly cautious and a time to reconsider your current situation."

Med's stomach sank. *Is she about to say we all failed?* Med felt an influx of terror as she tried to figure out what was coming next. *Maybe even reconsider this team.*

"No!" Med said.

The Mystics trained their eyes on her. Sweat dripped as she searched for the correct words. She felt like she was in a corner and needed to find the proper way out.

"Med, do you have something to add?" Solaria asked.

"Yes, I—" She hesitated. "I think there's something we can do."

Cyset looked at her with uncertainty. "Something?"

"I felt an unusual rush while we were dueling Argus. The power was incredible, and I saw my full potential," Med said.

"Your full potential?" Solaria asked. "Please continue."

Cyset turned to his mentor, still cautious.

Med had to think fast because she couldn't explain to Solaria that she had activated a power she never knew about, but at the same time, she needed to buy time so she wouldn't lose her position in Nexi Sciene. *What do I say? I can't fully lie to her, but what can I do to convince her?* She then remembered there was something she could do that her friends couldn't. Something she could probably do to Argus no one had ever tried.

"I believe I can heal Argus's mind."

Now everyone in the room had wide eyes, their full attention on her. Med took a breath and said, "I believe I can do this by fixing his mental instability."

Solaria walked toward Med. "Please follow me. There are people you need to meet."

Med followed her out of the room and down the hall. Med convinced herself she could talk her way through this.

***

Back in the office, the other Mystics were looking at one another, trying to figure out what was going on. Cyset leaned against the wall, arms folded glaring at the door trying to put together what he just heard. Jacks walked to him and pushed against his shoulder.

"Cy? Cy?" He tried again and again while Cyset thought. This time, Jacks shoved his arm. "Cy!" he nearly yelled.

Cyset snapped back to reality. He looked at Jacks. "Yeah?"

"The hell is going on right now?" Jacks asked. "Med's talking about healing Argus and we're just going to humor this idea as if that's not completely insane?"

"I can't stop her from saying something..." He trailed off as he noticed Dixie nervously bouncing her foot up and down while Scratch whispered to her.

"Cy?" Jacks asked.

"Give me a minute. I need to talk to Dixie and Scratch." He walked over to them and sat down next to Dixie. She looked over with pained eyes and gasped quietly.

"You should really tell someone when you're walking over. You startled me," Dixie said.

"Yeah, sorry, but just like you, I'm a little on edge," Cyset said.

"You look like it," Dixie returned.

Cyset shrugged it off and asked, "What happened in the alleyway?"

Dixie looked at Scratch and turned back to him.

"We saw Argus and we fended him off, that's all," Dixie said.

"Yeah, nothing more, nothing less," Scratch added.

"I didn't get everything you said before, Scratch, but I heard Med did something incredible in that story, so what happened?"

"Cyset, we can't exactly explain it," Dixie said.

"All right, but here's the thing, I can tell when someone is trying to save their ass. I would know because even I've tried lying to Solaria. I did stupid shit when I was younger, and I've learned about the consequences. So, what happened before Med does something she'll regret?"

Dixie sighed. "It was quick, but Med was in a rage and directed all of it toward Argus. He had Scratch and myself stuck in some sort of grip, so when we were down, we couldn't see what was going on. Med had control over most of the objects in the alley and created a cyclops."

"A what?" Cyset asked.

"Cyclops, you know, really—" Scratch said before Cyset raised his hand.

"I know what she said, but *what*?" Cyset said again.

"She did and she was about to squash him, but I stopped her and after I did, Argus started acting like she did something incredible," Dixie finished.

Cyset realized why Med made her statement. She had learned more about how powerful she was as a Dark Angel, but that didn't mean she could heal Argus.

He stood and walked over to a window, looking out at the city. His thoughts now were overloaded. Med had not only gone near mad but almost killed Argus in the process. She had used the ability to reinvent or convert objects, which could bring them to life or make them bend to the will of a Dark Angel's mind.

He didn't know what he would do about Med's outburst himself. He started to think of an answer and stopped himself. Every scenario made him more frustrated than the last. It was like banging his head against a steel wall; he needed to get around this issue without going back. It felt like trying to look at a painting sideways. How was he going to get through going forward? Cyset pondered these questions until Solaria and Med returned.

They entered the room together with Solaria keeping a hand on Med's shoulder and a hopeful demeanor. "It may have taken some extreme conversation," Solaria said. "However, I believe we've been able to come up with a very substantial plan of action."

Jacks leaned next to Cyset to whisper, "Is that a good or bad thing?"

Cyset raised his hand and motioned for him to keep quiet.

"Med's new surge from the energy we've been having may give us a distinct ability to track down Argus and stop him dead in his tracks. You will all continue to work on this issue and you will track down Argus and do everything in your power to heal him should you find him."

"Understood," Cyset replied, nodding.

"The blue hell are you—?" Before Jacks could finish, Cyset pinched the back of his neck.

"We can work around this issue," Cyset said, playing along to get information.

"Very well. I'll leave you be. Good luck to all of you," Solaria said as she walked away.

Cyset looked at Med, seemingly very uncomfortable, but didn't approach her with any intent. He simply looked around the room at his teammates and made a decision.

"Let's go back to the complex. I'm tired," he said.

CHAPTER 13

SEEKING ANSWERS

———

The next day in Complex 50 Site 3.23, Med sat on her bed holding her knees. She was trying her best not to freak out. She had told her friends and her idol a huge lie. She rocked back and forth, trying to keep herself in control. *Why did I do something so stupid? Why did I even think of that?* After a moment, she heard a knock at her door.

"Yes?" Med asked.

"It's Cyset. I need to ask you something."

Med got up and walked over to the door to greet him. As she opened the door, his yellow eyes locked with hers. She was incredibly nervous. She kept her composure as well as she could.

"Um, what's up?" Med asked.

"What's your plan for healing Argus?" Cyset asked.

"Oh, my plan is to get him to comply with us," Med said, sweat starting to run down her back. She wasn't moving as she waited for an answer.

Cyset finally nodded. "All right, but you need to give me something else."

"What?" Med asked.

"Like how? Argus is incredibly mentally disturbed. He threatened to corrupt Nexi Sciene when we were going after him. He wants to destroy the world we've set up. He hates Non-Mages and the idea of living in a world where we compromise with them."

Med quickly shut the door on him as she felt her heart beating out of her chest. She was exasperated. She went over to her bag and looked for anything that might help her out of her predicament. She knew Cyset must on the other side of the door, fuming, but she didn't have anything to tell him. He'd have to be upset for now. She pulled out a notebook she brought with her from home and began to review her training notes and how she could use her powers.

As she flipped through pages, words from training began to jumble and pile up in front of her. The words *control*, *stamina*, and *focus* began to echo throughout her mind. The ability to control her energy and move it to her hand; how she needed to build up stamina; she couldn't focus like she did before because it felt like instinct. She began to get overwhelmed and found a page about healing a disfigured person.

"Okay," she whispered aloud as she read. "'The Dark Angel's best ability when healing those who are cursed is to find a way to connect with their energy. Do not reconfigure nor readjust the user's magic. That will begin to change them permanently.'"

She dropped the notebook and shook her head at the thought. She knew that wasn't a way to fix the problem with Argus, nor was it an answer. She decided to flip through again and looked for one about how her energy worked. She read the page on energy and remembered how she was taught. She would be taken to an open space; somewhere similar to back home where only nature was around her. She didn't have a space near the ocean, but she could go to the woods behind the complex. There she could center her energy and her body to help her focus.

Med grabbed her notebook and put on her old training gear, black sweats, and a sleeveless violet shirt, and headed for the garage.

When she got outside, she bumped into Dixie and Shade, who were talking inside the garage.

"Whoa," Shade said.

"Hey, what's wrong?" Dixie asked.

Med couldn't say what she was going to do nor did she want to. "I, uh…" Med panicked. "I'm heading to the forest behind the complex to meditate is all." Med dashed out of the garage. She began sprinting as far into the forest as she could, running past the brightly colored leaves. The bright reds, oranges, greens, yellows, and pinks blitzed past her as she headed for a small area where the trees wouldn't grow.

Med collapsed there, breathing heavily, and looking around as her thoughts and questions washed over her. She took a deep breath and opened the notebook again. *Okay, come on, there's gotta be a way to fix Argus.* She went through everything taught to her about healing. The ability to heal, how to focus healing, the ability to heal trauma; anything that could make her lie become a truth.

She flipped through and watched words become mere fragmented symbols. As her stress built up, so did her magic. She began to lose control. It welled up and soon the book came to life and the pages flew off, swarming around her. She was stuck in a tornado of ink and dead tree. She was terrified as she saw the pages circle her as though they were a wall of crows attacking. Med cried out and caused the pages to fall to the ground in front of her. She screamed at the top of her lungs, causing the leaves to fall and rustle.

"This feels hopeless!" Med cried. "Why isn't there a way to heal Argus? Why didn't they just tell me about my powers? Why can't I figure any of this out right now?"

She sat in the area and tried to look up to the sky for an answer. She was lost.

CHAPTER 14

CONVERSATION

———

A night of sleep cleared none of the questions in Cyset's head. Even hours later in the afternoon of a new day, he didn't know what to make of what he had heard. All he wanted was to find out what exactly was going on. His teammate had lied, and his mentor had believed it. Med was supposedly going to heal one of the most dangerous people in Mystian.

His eyes focused on the ceiling, and it began to feel like it was hurtling toward him. The world caved in on him every time he began running the scenario and the options in his head, hoping to come up with an answer. He meditated, trying to relax, but nothing helped. He could not stand it any longer. Cyset rose from his bed and stretched before he walked out into the hallway and to Med's room. He needed answers, and he hadn't gotten them on his first attempt.

He walked up to Med's door and knocked on it. No answer.

"Med." He knocked again. "Med, I need to talk to you." Still no answer.

"She's not in her room," Shade said.

Cyset saw her standing outside of her room, arms folded. "Do you know where she went?"

"I saw her earlier, but she didn't say where she was going. You can try Dixie," Shade said

Cyset nodded. "Got it." He headed for the living room, where he found Dixie wrapping up a conversation on a call home. He walked over to where she was and tapped her shoulder.

"Oh, yeah. Love you too, Ma," Dixie said hanging up the phone. She turned to Cyset. "Hey, what'd ya need?"

"Do you know where Med is?" Cyset asked.

"Uh, she ran out of the garage and headed in the opposite direction from the base," Dixie said.

Cyset groaned. "All right, thanks." He turned to walk off when Dixie grabbed his arm.

"Look," Dixie said. "She's nervous and probably a little scared, so be understanding, not interrogating, all right?"

Cyset nodded as he headed for the garage. *I understand what she's doing—I just need to stop her before she gets too far along in her plan.* He groaned once more as he walked outside to the yard where Scratch was doing handstand pushups and calling out animal features. He was shouting "eyes of a hawk," "paws of a lion," and "skin of a reptile." It looked like he was trying to switch between his powers as quickly as he could.

"Hey, Scratch," Cyset called.

Scratch paused mid-handstand. "Hey, what's up?"

"I'm going to find Med."

"Oh, is she okay? Do you need a hand?" Scratch asked, jumping up.

"No, I'll be fine. Thanks." He stalked toward the forest. His mind plagued him as he walked. He passed by trees whose leaves glowed with their color. They were Pikeburns: trees that could create the illusion of a sky that held positive auras. The inner part of the forest was a mix of vibrant and cool colors with patches of shadow. Cyset felt like he was disturbing this pocket of serenity. He couldn't allow a moment of relaxation as he was trying to think.

He continued farther into the forest until he was engulfed in a purple sky and mist. His vision was a little compromised but not entirely lost. He kept going until he saw Med. She was sitting in a small area where the trees weren't fully surrounding her. There was an open area. Her eyes were closed, and her body was still as she sat meditating.

Cyset slowly walked up to her and sat down. "Med."

"Oh, hey," she said, opening her eyes.

"I need to talk to you about something," Cyset said.

Med looked away.

"You said you could heal Argus," he said, narrowing his eyes. "It's not a good idea to lie to Solaria when there's a serious issue going on."

"What?" she asked. "How did you know?"

"My mentor, while wise, is also willfully optimistic. She loves hearing good news and has grown to accept that over the years. I'm more interrogative, and I could tell from before in the training room that you have immense power but you need extreme focus to activate it, unless you're under intense stress."

"Okay, so you can read people?" Med asked.

"Yes. I look into people's problems and have been trained to understand and respond to those issues. That's why I'm in charge," Cyset said.

"Oh, so what are you trying to get out of me?"

"Why you're lying. If you're seriously gonna commit to this idea, you'll drive yourself crazy. I'm trying to make sure you don't do something reckless. Healing Argus could put you in serious danger."

"Being split from this team could be dangerous for me."

"Med, Argus knows how to send you over the edge. You saw what happened in that alley—imagine what will happen if he shows you more of what you can do," Cyset said.

"You know about that?" She jumped up, flustered.

Cyset remained seated. "I had an idea from Scratch and Dixie. Now I've got an answer. Why did you lie to Solaria?"

"I don't know! Unlike you, I'm not Solaria's protégé. Unlike Jacks, I can't go back to a mansion. Unlike a lot of you guys, I'll be sent back to my small town and forced to stay there."

"What, you think Solaria would really do that to you?"

"She's done it since I was born! How am I supposed to know she won't do it again?" Med asked. "Out of everyone, I don't want her to lose hope in what I can do."

Cyset had to hold off as he remembered the pressure that hit him as a kid and how being raised to be the best had overwhelmed him.

He had made mistakes trying to remain at the top of the charts and the head of everything. He needed to come clean if he was going to get Med to trust him and now wasn't the time to be the big Mystic but just another Mage. "I've lied to Solaria too."

Med she knelt in front of him. "You have?"

"Yes, when I was about sixteen. I did it so I could try and prove myself, and guess what, I almost did something I would regret." He let out a breath and thought hard on the memory. "I was adopted because my mother died in childbirth. I went out looking for a man I thought was my father and when I found him, I turned him into the Mystics' Operations Center. I wanted Solaria to declare what would happen to him since he abandoned a Mage, only to find out he wasn't my dad."

"You lied about that?"

"No, I lied saying I knew who my father was. In short, my father has no records and no evidence pointing to his existence, almost as if he doesn't exist."

She couldn't find the right words and instead stammered, "I just—why would you tell me any of this?"

"I thought I'd share first. Clearly whoever trained you didn't get to know you, but us? Me, Jacks, Dixie, Scratch, and Shade? We're all ears." Cyset hoped he'd made his point.

Med let out a small smile, and Cyset felt she was now more at ease and able to talk to him more.

"How touching." Argus's voice echoed from the sky.

Cyset and Med both jumped and looked around. They couldn't pinpoint where he was.

"So, you aren't afraid to confess your sins. Interesting," Argus said as he appeared on a path that led even farther away from the complex.

Med and Cyset stood firm.

"So, I don't know how to heal him, but do you know how to fight him?" Med whispered.

The young Wind Wizard grimaced. He could feel his head start to hurt. "Funny thing is, I do, but that just doesn't make it easier," he said, anticipating what would happen next.

CHAPTER 15

TRUST BUILDING

The old Dark Angel sneered at both of them, and his lifeless eyes held them in their grasp. What had been a simple hope to talk his friend down now became a moment of conflict with their newest foe. Cyset's energy built up inside him as he looked at Argus.

"So, Argus, what do you want now?" he asked. "A knuckle sandwich, your wisdom teeth knocked out, how about my foot up your—"

Argus raised his hand. "Please, please, I get the message."

"Do you? I don't think he does. Do you think he does?" Cyset said, turning to Med.

"Oh, look at you trying to be so buddy-buddy with your teammate," Argus said. "How touching."

"What? What are you trying to say this time?" Cyset asked.

"Don't you realize what she did? How much power she was able to pull? She could kill you without a second thought."

Cyset rolled his eyes.

"And what about you?" Med asked. "Can't you just destroy us?"

Cyset looked down and realized it was true. Why hadn't Argus tried to kill them?

"Good question, Med," Argus said. "Simply put, I'm old and looking for a successor. A *younger* successor."

"What?" she replied.

"Since when do people like you care about anyone else?" Cyset questioned.

"I care about what I believe in. I believe Dark Angels can alter reality if we agree to create it. We're a small number but so are the Light Angels. We can make something better if we just band together. If that means some people get hurt and some people are challenged, so be it," Argus said.

"Why? What would your New World Order do? You could get people killed, or worse, plunge people into infinite suffering. Chaos isn't the answer," Cyset argued.

Argus twisted his head sideways. "New World Order? No, no, no. It's more of a return to the *correct* order—an order where we survived because we had more Magical ability than the others."

Cyset had his ears and eyes turned up to ten. Argus was labeled as an anarchist, so what exactly was he talking about with his proclaimed old way of doing things?

"The heck does any of that mean?" Med asked.

"Hopefully, you'll get a chance to find out." He snapped his fingers and everything went black.

"Med? Med?" Cyset called, keeping his arms at a distance, hoping to touch something. Now he was in trouble.

As the world around her reformed, Med saw a different forest than before. The leaves were gone and the bark now black as pitch. The sky was pure white as she looked around and searched for any signs of a person. She didn't see Argus but she could hear him lurking nearby, laughing at her and mocking her for being so dazed. She called out, "Cyset?" She got no answer. She readied herself as something suddenly walked out.

"Med?" Cyset asked.

She was relieved as her friend appeared in front of her. She waved wildly to make sure he could see her. He ran over to her to see if she was all right, trotting up with vigor.

"Oh, my gosh, where are we?" she asked.

"Well…" He looked up. "If I were to guess, one of Argus's little reality scenarios."

"Scenarios? Like in the alleyway?" Med asked.

"Yeah. It's a power of his. He can create a new reality from wherever he is."

"That would've been cool to learn how to do," Med muttered under her breath. She didn't get a lot of time to think about it as they heard some rustling from the trees. "What was that?"

"Knowing our luck, nothing good," Cyset said. Dealing with the day before up to now was a good indicator. The rustling revealed some dark branch figures popping out of the woods. Tall and very lanky, they looked like strange tree-branch men. A combination of sap and mud walked toward the two Mages.

"It looks like we're going to have to fight those, aren't we?" Med asked.

"Yeah, looks like it," Cyset said, getting into a defensive stance. "You ever been in a fight?"

"Do you count the one in the alleyway?" Med asked.

"All right, so not a lot. Well, get ready to put training into practice—we're gonna be up against a heck of a lot."

"Okay, got it," she said as the figures sprinted toward them.

"Stay close!" Cyset yelled.

Med moved behind him as he pushed air out from his hands. This blast knocked the figures to the ground, disrupting their charge.

"Quick, get some distance from me. If we're too bunched up, we won't be able to move well," he said as the two of them began moving and sliding around, trying to stay out of the reach of the figures. One started throwing his sharpened limbs at Med. She avoided it before receiving a scratch on her right arm.

She nervously forced magic into her arms and allowed them to shield her for a moment. She closed her eyes and wildly shot from her left hand. The punch was infused with her powers and paid off as the figure tumbled backward. Another popped up on her right, forcing her to duck another swing of branches before throwing another punch with her right hand. This one didn't fall but it was put off balance. Med made a beeline for a rock to get some distance between them.

She got a glimpse of Cyset using his wind to blow back a figure before wind-jumping over one and kicking it in the back of the head. He rolled over to Med who was trying to keep her wits about her.

"You okay?" he asked.

She nodded. "I don't really know what I'm doing right now. It feels like autopilot."

"You're not dead, so you're doing great, but we need a way to get this over with," Cyset said.

"Wait! Maybe I can try something. In the alleyway, I was able to manipulate reality before and when I did, Argus was knocked on his butt and lost power. Maybe I can try and take it a step further enough to disrupt his control."

The Wind Wizard smiled as he saw the figures getting together for another charge. "Here's what you need to do.

Like when you heal, build up your energy and then release it. This time, focus your energy as if you're holding a breath and then blowing out."

"Okay." Med began to control her energy. She focused it into her arms before opening her eyes once more. The aura on her body was a lilac purple as she looked forward, extended her arms, and expelled a wash of extreme energy around her and Cyset.

This energy expanded, and the world was engulfed in white as they were transported back to the original setting of the forest where Argus was standing in place of the figures.

"Impossible," Argus said, dazed.

Cyset immediately threw him into a tree with a push of air. "Not so."

Med pulled her arms back and stared at her hands. *Whoa, I thought that was going to make me turn like Argus, but it didn't. In fact, I feel incredible!*

Argus stood up, rattled by Cyset's gust of wind and the impact of hitting the tree. He was angry and foaming at the mouth.

"Damn you! Damn you both!" he screamed as he faded into the darkness once more.

Med jumped after him before Cyset grabbed her.

"Hey, whoa, whoa. It's cool. He's not worth following without the others anyway," he said, meeting her eye.

Med pulled back and eased up. She looked again at her hands and then to Cyset. "I, well—" She paused before continuing. "That may have been the first real magic I've ever done."

"You know," he said, wiggling his index finger, "I think maybe what we need as a team is a quick meeting."

Med raised an eyebrow and nodded.

CHAPTER 16

TEAM BUILDING

————

Med and Cyset headed back to Complex 50, Site 3.23. Med was quiet. She had no idea what Cyset was thinking and couldn't put together what he was going to say. *What is he going to bring up?* Her thoughts raced. She decided maybe she should just ask a question. "Uh, Cyset?"

"Hmm?" he responded.

"What exactly are you planning to do when we get to the complex?"

"Well." He put his hand to his head. "I think the best idea would be to give the others an idea of what's been going on. You have to tell them you lied."

"What?" she shrieked.

"Hey, they deserve to know what's going on."

"How am I supposed to explain that?" Med was horrified at the idea.

"Trust me, I'll have your back the entire time," Cyset said, continuing forward.

Med sighed. The two kept walking until the entrance to the forest appeared in front of them. Med felt her heart rate spike.

Oh, no. The two arrived at the complex and she felt a series of knots in her stomach. She felt like the door was some sort of portal to hell.

Cyset's hand met her shoulder. "Hey, like I said, we all make mistakes. Nothing new."

Med sighed and nodded. The two walked through the garage to the living room. Med kept telling herself she needed to be honest with her teammates. When they entered the living room, they found them playing *Go Fish*.

"Hey, guys," Cyset said.

The Mystics turned their heads, and Med once again felt knots pulling inside of her body. Dixie and Scratch looked relieved. Jacks and Shade looked concerned.

"So, where'd you two go?" Shade asked.

"Forest. We ran into Argus, and we need to let something be known." Cyset turned to Med and nodded.

She stepped forward with her heart pounding and body shaking. Her mind raced as she found the words. Cyset once again put a hand on Med to steady her as she began to speak.

"I, uh—" She swallowed hard. "I lied about what I can do for Argus." She turned red as she told them what she had done. They stared at her. She turned to Cyset, who gave her two thumbs up with a bit of a crooked smile. She didn't feel at ease, but her heart was slowing down.

"That's quite the lie," Dixie said.

Scratch nodded.

"Damn. I thought *I'd* done stupid shit before," Jacks said before receiving a punch to the arm.

Shade was just smiling wickedly.

"Why are you so happy?" Cyset asked, glaring at her.

"Because I think that's the most relatable thing I've heard out of any of you," Shade said, leaning back in her chair. She winked at Med.

"Look, I don't know why I did it. I felt nervous, and Solaria was talking about a new type of team. Then she started looking at all of us, and I didn't want to go home. I thought I was gonna lose my chance and all of a sudden I just said—" Before she could finish, Cyset and Dixie tried to steady her.

"Okay. Breathe, breathe," said Dixie, talking her down.

"Sorry," Med choked out.

"Pssh, you think you're the first person to lie to do something?" Jacks asked.

"What?" Med looked at him.

"I lied to my personal Sage and almost burned down my home trying to learn something I wasn't ready for," said Jacks, chuckling. "My dad was pretty mad."

"I lied to a Mystic on the street about what I could do to enter a Mystic building when I was fifteen. I was trying to see what the big deal was. Ended up almost getting put in juvenile detention only to be saved by Solaria," Shade chimed in, shaking her head.

"I lied to a snake once. He believed me," Scratch mentioned.

Med turned to Cyset. He was smirking and shrugging his shoulders.

"Like I said, we all do it at least once," he said.

Med let out a sigh of relief before being able to stand up. "I guess I kind of got a little... anxious."

"Nothing wrong with that. Everyone gets anxious when they're put under pressure," Dixie comforted.

"You are not alone in your problems," Cyset said.

Med was elated. The comfort from her fellow Mages was wonderful. Her heart began to swell with relief and joy. It overwhelmed her. She felt a sense of hope until the moment was interrupted by Jack's phone. It went off like a gunshot.

"Uh, give me a moment," Jacks said, walking out of the room to take the call.

Med looked around at the others as he walked into the hallway. She saw Shade fold her arms.

"Bet it's just some sort of robocall," she joked.

Scratch and Dixie shrugged but Cyset looked concerned. Med took that as a sign of things to come. Jacks came bursting back into the room.

"You all need to hear this." Jacks set the phone on the table with the speaker enabled.

Argus's voice met them, causing Med's body to chill. Her anxiety returned as she heard his voice.

"Hello, Mystics of Complex 50, site 3.23. You are being invited to the Asinoc Olayer hotel. This is not an invitation you will want to miss. You will learn about your world and your history as Mages in a way you've never gotten to experience, and when it is all over, you will then become something more than just pawns—you will be free to move on and out of the board." The phone went silent as the call cut out.

The moment of relief had passed for Med as she stared at the phone. Adrenaline rushed over her. "This is a trap, isn't it?"

"Oh, yeah." Cyset groaned. "But we can't just let him go messing with people in the Asinoc Olayer."

"What do you think he wants?" Shade questioned.

"Don't know," said Jacks. "I don't care what he wants anyway."

"I take it we're all in agreement?" Dixie motioned.

"Unanimously," Scratch said, nodding. "Let's rip him apart."

Med made a fist and felt the magic in her body burn as she readied herself. She wasn't going to run from Argus. Not anymore.

CHAPTER 17

GLASS HOUSE

———

Med and her teammates arrived at the Asinoc Olayer. The building was lit up with intense energy. The building was high, and Med tried to scale the amount of energy. Cyset and Jacks ran ahead toward the door. She quickly followed as they gathered around it. Cyset blew open the door, hoping to find Argus, and got his wish immediately. Argus sat at the concierge desk.

"Hmm," Argus hummed. "You accepted my invitation. Thank you."

Med's powers kicked in instinctively. She was seeing red. Argus had been driving her and her friends up a wall and now he had the nerve to try and talk down to them.

"What do you want now?" Cyset questioned.

"I want to give you a lesson, since it seems none of you understand." Argus floated off the desk to a balcony above it. "Of course, I am a horrible lecturer. Why don't we do this visually?" he said as his veins glowed purple once more. This time, the floor and environment around the Mystics cracked like thin ice.

"Oh, come on," Shade groaned.

The floor, walls, chandelier, and world seemed to collapse around Med and her friends as they fell. She thought she would fall forever until being grabbed by Cyset, who was able to fly with his wind abilities.

"Whoa, I gotcha," he called, holding tightly.

Med turned her head to see Jacks grab Dixie's hand. Scratch flew overhead, flapping his arms like a bird.

"Uh, why?" she asked, confused at what Scratch was doing.

"To use the magic I have to imitate the movements of some animals," he explained. "It's the joy and curse of my powers."

That explains a lot.

"Hey, wait," Dixie exclaimed. "Where's Shade?"

"Over here!" Shade said, seemingly standing on air.

"Let me guess, your powers allow you to—" Cyset started before Shade cut in.

"Stand anywhere and move freely because this world is technically a shadow. Yeah," Shade said, arms folded.

"No talking during the lesson!" Argus screamed through the void.

Med searched for Argus. She couldn't put together where he was or what he was doing, but unlike before, she couldn't feel his presence. After a moment, she looked up to see a platform made of glass.

"Guys, up there!" Med said. The others looked up at the panes of light.

"Going up," Cyset said, levitating to the glass. He put Med down as they settled.

She saw a blue streak follow them onto the glass. She squeaked slightly with fright before the streak turned into Shade, traveling in the shadows. She let out a breath and looked down. The platform they were standing on was a glass pane showing an image of Light Angels talking to people.

A tale that had been passed down in all histories, the Light Angels were the first Mages to appear and the first to reach out to Non-Mages. It was always said they worked to keep peace. The people were shown worshipping the Light Angels.

"The hell?" Cyset whispered as he looked down at the image.

"Do you recognize this?" Argus questioned. "This is the beginning, but why don't you examine closely? Are the Light Angels talking to or commanding these people?"

Jacks, Dixie, and Scratch showed up, looking at the glass floor as well.

"Just because you say it doesn't make it true!" Shade yelled into nothing.

"Keep jumping between the murals, children," Argus said.

Med could see a small vein protruding from Shade's face. She latched onto Cyset as the team headed for another mural above them. They hopped on. The image was a magenta-haired Light Angel wearing a long robe and speaking with a being; a Dark Angel, small and wearing more aggressive clothing and armor. They were clearly in disagreement about something. The mural showed several symbols, all of them unrecognizable and foreign to Med. She wasn't alone. Her teammates clearly had no idea what any of these meant either.

"How about this image? Does it tell you anything?"

"You already know the answer to that, Bone Man. What are you trying to prove?" Cyset yelled.

"Oh, really? Maybe you didn't learn anything. How about this one?" Argus yelled as another image fell down. This one represented most Mystics' Operation Centers. It was of a Light Angel holding all the Mage symbols; a sign meant to represent how Light Angels were the current leaders of the Mage world. Also showing how all Mages revered and respected them. "Light Angels currently hold all the Mages together. Does none of this make you angry?"

"What is with you?" Jacks replied. "There's nothing wrong with them leading! What are you trying to be?"

"The cure?" Scratch asked.

"The answer?" Dixie screamed.

"You mock me, but right now you are left to my rules and my world, so you will get the message!" Argus echoed as the murals now made a huge grand floor surrounded by water. Argus appeared on the far side of the floor, yet his voice was as clear as if he was standing right in front of the group. "I've been showing you history as it unfolded: Light and Dark Angels ruled over everything and the Light Angels, in a moment of weakness, agreed to help those without our abilities."

"What? Living in harmony is a bad thing?" Cyset yelled so Argus could hear him.

"Living like a Non-Mage when you are a Mage is like pretending to be an ant when you are a giant," Argus returned. "This is what Mages are meant to be: beings that fight for power like Gods high on their mountain."

Med thought she would vomit.

"All in favor of kicking this guy in the face say 'aye,'" Shade called.

"Aye!" Med and the others responded.

Argus kneeled on the glass his head down.

"Is that a surrender?" Dixie joked.

"No, this is my declaration of war," Argus said. Power pulsed from his hand and spread throughout the entire floor. The glass rose. On every side, a wave of polygonal monsters surrounded the perimeter. They all reflected varying colors from wherever they were, ranging from pastel to bright and flashy neon.

"Welp, he has an army... but he did say he was going to war," Scratch said.

Med looked to Argus but he was gone. Argus was ascending the water slowly and methodically. His arms outstretched. He ascended above them.

"No, you don't!" Med cried as she ran after him.

"Med!" Cyset yelled as she sprinted forward, using her energy to take some of the figures out of her path. She didn't care what he said as she began to chase after Argus. This time, she thought of the way to get after him. Abusing the energy he had set up, she shifted the reality to make a staircase. She climbed up the staircase, focused solely on stopping Argus. She found herself getting higher and higher until what seemed to be a glass man appeared before her. She got ready. Her mind told her to attack. Her body said she should be still. Bam! The figure was struck down by fire. Med looked down to see Jacks winking before moving out of the way of other polygonal figures.

Med continued up the steps she was making, hoping to cut off Argus. Another glass man appeared. She stopped, ready to take it on, but Scratch flew up to the staircase. He pounced onto the figure and held it to the ground.

"If you can get Argus, get Argus. We'll handle the Mural Monsters," he yelled before flipping it off the steps.

Med nodded and continued forward. She saw Shade's blue streak right next to her. The figures tried to climb up to the next steps. Shade moved ahead and suffocated that area in shadow until the figures were falling back to the ground. Med sprinted and another figure appeared. She had no allies to help her this time.

"Med, duck!" Cyset called. She squatted down as he floated up, carrying Dixie. Dixie then tackled a Prism monster off the steps after Cyset flew by hovering over. She ran over to see if Dixie was all right but she jumped back up on one of the floors.

"Whew, that was fun!" Dixie exclaimed.

Med let out a sigh of relief before being tugged by Cyset.

"Hey, come on. There's a way out. Let's go." Cyset pointed to the door at the top of the stairway. She ran with him and they burst through the door into the access stairway of the hotel. They ran up the flight to find the exit to the roof. Med reached for the door only to be stopped dead in her tracks by Cyset.

"Argus can't get away!" Med shouted.

"Yeah, he can't get away, but how do you plan on stopping him?" Cyset said. "You can't do it alone, but the team can. What do we do to get them out of the illusion? If we don't, they'll be fighting polygon monsters all night."

Well, his focus needs to be disrupted.

"Okay, so one clean shot on his head oughta do it?" Cyset asked.

"Probably the best option we have," Med said.

Cyset let out a sigh before looking at Med directly in the eyes. "Just so you know, when we grab him, you will have to talk to Solaria, since you can't heal him."

Med nodded. "Well, that's why you'll have my back." She punched Cyset in the shoulder.

He smiled. "You ready?"

"I believe I am," Med said. "Now more than ever."

"Let's do it."

CHAPTER 18

RUMBLING ROOFTOP PART 1

———

The rooftop of the Asinoc Olayer was quite big. It was known for having a helipad and a beautiful view of the city's skyline. Cyset led Med around the observation area. He checked the areas around them, hoping to keep them unseen. He motioned for her to get closer and peered around the corner. All clear. He began to walk up to the top of the roof, looking back to make sure Med was following closely. He found the stairs that led to the helipad on the roof and knelt to stay out of sight. Once there, he and Med would be facing down Argus. He knew what was coming next and began to muster his energy in preparation for the confrontation.

"Okay, we're checking the helipad," he said as he laced up one of his sneakers to make sure it was extremely tight.

"He knows we're coming after him," Med said.

"I'd be surprised if he didn't think we were," Cyset said, getting himself ready.

Cyset motioned for Med to follow him up and the two found the helipad empty. Med looked for anything on the ground and ran to the edge of the roof. Cyset felt like his head was going to burst from the stress.

"What? But—" Med knelt, frustrated, and put her hands to her face. "Where can he go?"

Before she asked anything else, Cyset noticed Argus's silhouette calling forth energy. "Get back!" Cyset yelled.

Cyset ran over to Med and saw her head jerk back, narrowly missing multiple sharp projectiles.

"What, what's wrong?" Med asked. She turned to see Argus standing at the other end of the helipad.

He was livid. There was no crooked smile, no silly expression—no toying. The Dark Angel had truly embraced his cold, hollow soul and was now ready to unleash its wrath. His presence was undoubtedly instilled with rage and chaos. His body glowed vibrantly with his energy sparking and striking.

"I have had enough of this," he snarled.

Cyset activated his energy and looked over at Argus. His sight was set on finding some sort of weak point to knock out Argus's concentration.

"Last chance to surrender, Skullman. Take your pick," he called to him. Cyset felt the floor below him shake and lift as he looked down before being ejected into the air. He was spinning and being flung around as he kept flying through the sky. He caught a glimpse of another object before being hit straight in the face by it. Cyset could taste blood. He had to correct himself or suffer his face getting hit again. He used his magic to blow himself back to the ground before levitating there.

Cyset landed, spitting blood out of his mouth. Argus mustered his energy and Cyset pushed him back with his magic, allowing Med to grab his arms and hold him against the wall Argus had built. Cyset sprinted and locked his knee over the back of Argus's left leg, pinning him down. He held Argus's face on the ground.

"You will listen to me!" Argus said.

"I don't fall for lies," Cyset said before wrapping his arm around Argus's neck to restrain him. As he began to force his knee down, Argus threw up his head and connected with Cyset's face. Cyset reeled from the impact while Argus attempted to stomp him. Cyset's instinct made a gust that pushed Argus into the air.

"Ow." Med groaned, holding her torso.

"What happened?" Cyset asked.

"He used his head to hit me in the stomach," Med said. "He made his neck extend like a giraffe or something."

"Yeah, he hits hard, despite looking like a diseased old man," Cyset said.

Argus floated above them and unleashed a wave of energy at them. Cyset tackled Med to make sure she wasn't hit. She put her hand up, creating an energy field around the two of them.

"Dang it, how can he do that?" she asked.

"Wisdom comes with experience and unfortunately, he has quite a bit." Cyset thought for a moment as he saw the energy around them begin to wane and fade. "I think I can bring him back to Earth, but you're going to have to be ready. When I give you a signal, drop the shield and I'll try and rush him in the air."

"Yeah, whatever works," Med said, struggling to keep the forcefield intact.

"Okay, drop the shield on three!" Cyset kneeled and charged his powers.

Argus kept raining down energy and the onslaught grew more intense. His blasts were hitting harder, and Cyset could feel something worse was coming.

"One." He looked up as Argus reeled back. "Two." He waited. Argus stopped and pulled his arm up. "Three!" he yelled.

Med dropped the shield, and Cyset practically flew into the air. He rammed right into Argus's chest with his knee before pulling in Argus's head and falling to the ground with him. As they fell, Cyset lessened his impact while Argus hit the ground hard. Cyset managed to get up and pull Argus from the ground, holding his arms behind his back and locking his legs in place.

"Now, Med!" he called, keeping Argus as still as he could.

Cyset watched Med run up and deliver a punch with a huge amount of force perfectly on the side of Argus's head. Cyset smiled as Argus staggered from the impact before flinging him aside. Argus bounced across the ground, dazed, and stunned.

"Hey, I didn't break my hand!" Med cried, rubbing her first two knuckles.

"Awesome," Cyset said. He turned to Argus, who stood up and then fell to his knees, the air taken from him and his breath sporadic. The walls he had built were gone and the helipad open to be seen by everyone once more. Argus was in a fit of rage on the ground. Cyset was pleased with the result. He turned away wiping his forehead. All he needed to do now was wait for the others; until he felt a hand on his back.

Argus grabbed him by the back of his shirt and threw him straight into Med. The Dark Angel then skated over to them, this time grabbing them both by the necks before throwing them down again.

"I refuse to be beaten by the prodigy of a harlot and the disgrace of an entire Mage class!" Argus spat, forcing the two to the earth. Cyset felt Argus's energy enter his body. In the same way that Med could heal, it seemed Argus could do the opposite.

Cyset did everything he could to rip Argus off him, but nothing worked; it was as though Argus had turned himself into a piece of metal to hold himself in place.

Please, tell me this is not how I die. He ran out of air and energy before he saw Argus take a fireball to the side of his face. Argus dropped them, and Cyset grabbed Med and flew back to the other side of the helipad.

"Hey, you try and do that to my best friend and I will freaking kill you!" Jacks yelled, with his hands on fire. Cyset took a knee trying to catch his breath, until Med put a hand on him and restored his oxygen. The other Mystics had joined them.

"Is the hotel back to normal?" he asked, getting to his feet.

"Yeah, it changed back a few moments ago," Jacks said.

"So, what took you guys so long?" Cyset asked.

"We were on the first floor, the roof is fifty flights up, and we had to take the elevator," Jacks said, embarrassed.

Cyset glanced at Med, making sure she was okay. She gave him a thumbs up and he then saw Argus begin to get up, foaming at the mouth and snarling like a rabid animal.

"I will tolerate you nitwits no longer!" Argus cried.

"He's pissed," Jacks snarked.

Cyset nudged his shoulder to indicate holding off on the remarks so they could figure out how to take on Argus. "Yeah, and he's not showing any remorse, either. It's going to take a lot to get this dude down."

Argus howled as though charging up everything inside of him.

"Well, here we go with this," Cyset said and readied into a charging stance.

There was nothing more to do than engage Argus. If they ran, Argus would just come hunting them down. This was the best option. It was time to stop Argus or leave him to his devices.

CHAPTER 19

RUMBLING ROOFTOP PART 2

———

The adrenaline running through Cyset was overwhelming as he kept avoiding and gliding around the helipad to keep Argus at bay. The Dark Angel had gone fully off the deep end and now decided to show off his power. Argus seemed determined to make sure the Mystics understood his power. He had been fighting them for at least half an hour or so, bouncing fire off himself and directing energy anywhere he could. Argus flung Scratch off his arm and Cyset slid over to a sweating Jacks.

"All right, this has been going on for some time," Jacks panted.

"Well, like I said, he's pretty mad." Cyset felt like he had been fighting Argus for a year because of how much energy he had thrown around. Dixie and Shade ran toward Argus in an attempt to tackle him, and turning, he caught Med working on Scratch and made a decision. It would cost him, but if he didn't go with it, he could very well be in trouble.

"Keep blasting him. I've got an idea," he told Jacks before sprinting off. He flipped, slid, and flew over the scattered pieces of debris. He landed next to Med and Scratch. "Hey, time for more power."

Med looked at him. He knew he had to choose his next words carefully.

"Look, I'm not saying do everything he does. I'm saying use just enough to throw off his mojo so we can get ours," Cyset said.

"None of that made sense to me. All I know is I've done that twice; once in an alleyway and the second time in the forest. Every time I do, I feel like I'm getting lucky."

"Yeah, maybe, but it's better than just praying he'll go down," Cyset said.

Med nodded and looked over to Argus, who was firing energy at Shade and Dixie. They were hiding behind rocks trying not to get obliterated. She knelt and prepped her magic.

"Remember, just throw him off with anything you can," Cyset said.

He watched as Med caused an image to form from behind her. The image took shape and lo and behold, it was Solaria— at least, some form of her. He was awestruck. It was amazing, not only because he saw Solaria, but it had her bright aura glowing around her. *Huh. That's not what I expected.* The image flew to stand before Argus. Argus rescinded his attack as the image made him quiver in fear.

Cyset saw an opening and took it. He bolted toward Argus, punching him in the face before skidding and coming back around. He saw Scratch slash, Dixie punch, and Jacks fly toward Argus. Cyset tripped him, and Shade proceeded to hold Argus down with her shadows. He struggled to break free as the image of Solaria floated down and aimed a burst of light directly upon his body.

Argus screamed an ungodly scream one more time as he finally passed out from his struggling. Cyset smiled when Argus was finally down.

Med dropped to her hands too. He rushed to her and helped her up.

"Med, Med!" he cried.

"Ah, I'm exhausted, please." She paused. "No yelling."

"Sorry." He smiled. "Nice move. How'd you do that?"

"I just thought about my hopes and ambitions and I guess that popped out," Med said.

Cyset nodded, grinning from ear to ear as he couldn't believe Argus was down. His elated smile returned to serious business when he saw a Mystic ship fly over and land on the roof. Out walked Solaria.

"What in the name of Mystian's magic happened here?" She gasped, looking at them.

"Oh." Cyset sighed. "This is gonna be a headache."

***

Inside of the Mystics' Operations Center, Med waited with a pulsing heartbeat and surge of adrenaline. The rush from her fight with Argus had not worn off and she was incredibly anxious. Solaria wanted to speak with her, and Med would have to explain how she lied. Solaria walked through the door of the small office. Med took a breath and got ready.

"Good evening," Solaria said. Med nodded. "Argus has been brought here to the Mystic Operation Center."

Med swallowed hard.

"However, he seems to be more damaged than healed, to which I must ask, what exactly happened?"

Med took a breath and gathered herself. "Ma'am, I have something to confess." She looked her dead in the eyes. "I lied to you. I-I have no idea how to heal Argus whatsoever."

"You lied to me about your abilities?"

"Yes."

"You realize being a Mystic is not the same thing as being any other job professional, correct?"

"Yes." Med started to sweat.

"My question now becomes…" Solaria paused before continuing. "Why would you think you had to lie to me about your abilities?"

Med couldn't believe what she heard. "Aren't you mad?"

"That all depends on what you tell me next," Solaria said, putting her hand on Med's shoulder. "Because your teammates have described you as incredible and irreplaceable after what you've done. You've ascended, you've amazed them, you've astonished them, and you've even greatly impressed one of them, in their words."

"But, again, I-I lied to you," Med squeaked.

"So have others," said Solaria, standing up. "But they lied about how they perceived me. They lied to get something out of me, never to try and keep my respect."

Med thought about her next words carefully. "I lied out of fear that I wasn't going to be a Mystic anymore, or I was going to be kicked off this team," she admitted. Her hands were clasped together. She was ashamed to admit her fears. She felt weak and insecure in front of her idol.

"I don't change Mystic teams after assigning them," Solaria said. "I assign them based on what I believe will be best, and the paperwork and personal troubles would be extremely time-consuming."

Med was both relieved and a little confused. She wanted to think that everything was fine, but this explanation felt hollow. She believed in Solaria, no question, but her mind would not allow her to think of everything that had happened as some strange coincidence of events.

"So, what happens now if there is no problem?" Med asked.

Med could see Solaria was trying to find a way to phrase her next sentence.

"Now," said Solaria. "Now, I believe you should head back to the complex with your friends and rest. I do believe you will have to be on probation, but I won't remove you from your team. It clearly seems you've found a home."

Med nodded.

"And, Med."

She looked up at Solaria with wide eyes.

"I am impressed by your growth."

Med's heart exploded. She was elated because those were the words she needed to hear. She smiled from ear to ear, bowing multiple times.

"Thank you!" she cried. She tried to contain her excitement. "Uh, ahem, thank you, Ma'am. I'll do that." She turned around and looked at Solaria once more. "One last thing."

"Yes?"

"What are you going to do about Argus?"

Solaria's brow lowered. "He'll need a very thorough investigation into his disappearance, starting with an interrogation I'll be seeing to personally."

Med nodded and proceeded calmly out of the door and into the hallway. Her shoulders relaxed and her mind was at ease. She didn't have to worry about Argus; all she had to worry about was getting to her room and resting.

Med clicked a button to summon the elevator. She walked in and began jumping for joy inside. She was over the moon. She had impressed her idol and been able to let go of her fear.

"This is the best!" she screamed as the elevator continued down the building to the ground floor.

CHAPTER 20

INTERROGATION

———

Cyset waited outside of the holding area for Solaria. He was antsy and his mind raced. *Come on, come on, the longer we wait, the more time he has to think of a lie.* He knew Argus had a way to escape from the cell. After all, if he could disappear, what kept him from doing so again? He tapped his feet impatiently until he saw Solaria walking up to the room he was in. He stood up straight.

"Be at ease, Cyset," Solaria said.

He nodded and they turned to look at the door. "Does he know you personally?" Cyset asked. There was a moment of pause. He continued, "It's just that he brought up your name. I wouldn't think anything of it unless you knew him."

"Yes, we have a bit of a history."

Cyset's eyes went wide and he shivered.

"Believe me, after today, I hope to bury our history knowing he will be locked away in here," Solaria assured him.

Cyset wasn't so sure, but he remained stoic. Solaria opened the door with her handprint and they walked into a pure white holding area. Argus sat before them. In pure light, it was clear just how deformed he was. He was a dead man walking. The hatred inside of his lifeless, sunken eyes aimed at Cyset. He felt them trying to penetrate his spirit and suck the life out of him.

Argus shifted his gaze away and proceeded to look at Solaria. Cyset found a small patch of wall and leaned against it. He stared Argus down as he watched the old man shift in his chains, trying to get a lock on Solaria and snarl in her direction.

"So," Argus rasped. "The witch has descended from her hiding place."

While he knew striking a chained man was cowardly, Cyset felt his body tense up. He was ready to show Argus the darkest parts of his soul as he moved forward. Solaria raised her hand and Cyset stopped. *I'll end him if he says something like that again.*

"Your venom is as ineffective as ever, snake. Maybe that is why you fail once more at poisoning your prey."

"Once more?" Cyset whispered, listening.

Solaria bent to look Argus deep in the eyes. "Yet, I wonder… You claim I descend, but where did you crawl from?"

Argus squinted and began to smile crookedly. "I see you still try your best to look thirty-one at most. How many years are you again?"

"Never ask a woman her age," Solaria asserted. "How about you? Two, maybe three hundred?"

Argus bit his tongue and spit blood at the two of them.

"Despicable as ever."

"Prim and proper with no substance," Argus scoffed. "No wonder Mages have gone to hell."

"We are not gods, Argus!"

"Aren't we? Can't a god burn a man with his finger?"

"You speak of power and no mercy."

"Can't that be a ruler?"

"Isn't it a menace?"

Cyset listened, intrigued. *Why is he comparing us to gods?* Cyset had never thought of his magic as a bargaining tool.

"So, where do you think I went?" Argus said, rolling back to look at the ceiling.

"Probably somewhere foul. It would fit you," Solaria said as she circled his cell.

"'Foul' isn't the word I'd use." Argus closed his eyes and smiled. "It was nirvana; peace, a place of meditation and a moment isolated from time." His smile grew to a frown as he opened his eyes again. "I learned on that island, and I remembered what could be if you hadn't made deals and sold us to compromise."

"An absolute is not a solution."

"Maybe you just fear the thought of us isolating ourselves for freedom of choice."

Cyset started to put together what Argus meant. "You couldn't be found in any major city, so you took refuge in an isolated area?" he questioned getting both Solaria and Argus's attention.

"Scary how easily I can slip away, isn't it?" Argus sneered. His bitterness was palpable, and Cyset was getting a bit of a kick out of making him angry.

"Might be, but that's not what I care about." He walked over and knelt in front of Argus. "Though I'll ask you this: why are you so adamant on teaching Med what you know?"

Argus looked at Cyset's eyes and for the first time, his face showed that of pity. "You're a Wind Wizard. Your mark lives in your eyes, and yet one of the most beautiful marks, those yellow irises, are marred with white blinding fog."

Cyset paused. He hadn't heard Argus speak like that. He wasn't going to show him pity now, not after what he tried to do to him and his friends. "Beautiful words from such a demented soul," he said before getting up and walking out of the room.

He waited outside for Solaria. He had expected her to immediately follow; granted, he still thought about what he had heard. Argus was incredibly infatuated with the thought of being a god, but more importantly, why did he talk to Solaria like she was the reason he wasn't? Argus painted Solaria like she was corrupt. Why should he believe Argus? Argus was a criminal. A terrorist; yet, he was unwavering in his dedication to convince Cyset and his friends about the past.

Finally, Solaria came out of the room. She looked annoyed by the conversation she'd had.

"What happened in there?" Cyset asked.

Solaria brushed her hair back. "Well, he was stubborn about his little escapade, but it seems he disappeared to an island full of Mages."

"And?" he questioned.

"Just Mages. No one else at all."

This was a first for Cyset. He had never heard of something like that. Mages had always lived with Non-Mages. Since when was there an island for just Mages?

"Are you sure he wasn't lying to you?"

"As I've said, I've got a bit of a history with Argus. I can say he's never held back."

Cyset kept that in mind as he simply nodded. "So, are we going to go looking for this island?" He was concerned and ambitious. "I mean, we don't know if he has some sort of army or little cult he's formed over there."

Solaria placed a hand on Cyset's shoulder to reassure him. "That island is going to be hard to investigate. Getting information and Sages to also join would be hard. Thankfully, we have Argus in a cell where he can't hurt anybody. His magic won't be of any use in that room with nothing to manipulate but himself. For now, we take our victories as they come and focus on preventing more problems."

"Are you sure?" Cyset asked.

"I am deadly sure this will be fine." Solaria looked at the door. "If Argus and his army were united, they would have come with him on this run."

"Right," Cyset answered, but he didn't feel any better about the idea.

"You and your friends have been going through a lot, but you haven't had a lot of time to get to know each other. Maybe you should set up something fun to do after all of this."

Cyset looked at Solaria with a raised eyebrow and a devious smile. "We can do anything?"

Solaria raised a finger. "Anything you're legally allowed to do."

"Of course," Cyset said.

Solaria smiled as she walked away. "Have a good evening, sweetie."

"Right," Cyset said as he walked over to the elevator. He got on immediately and headed to the ground level. He pondered what he should do if Argus escaped. He came to a decision about it: he would have him and his friends waiting for Argus as a collective unit long before Argus got a chance to do anything. For now, he knew exactly where he was taking his teammates to relax.

After the elevator dinged, he headed for the garage. He was content with the idea that, instead of tensing up about what to do about Argus, he would simply get himself ready;

ready to strike, ready for a breakout, and ready for anything coming his way.

CHAPTER 21

FINAL THOUGHTS

—

Med sat in her room, giving herself a moment to breathe and think as she reflected on everything that had just happened. Breathe in, breathe out. She was enjoying the quiet after the chaos. Her mind was free to be alone with her thoughts, giving her a sense of relaxation until she heard a knock at her door.

"Who's there?" Med asked.

"Cyset."

Med walked over to her door and found her friend standing with his hands in the pocket of a hoodie. The hoodie had the caption *Walking Tornado* on it, and Cyset was more relaxed than before. His shoulders were lowered and his brow relaxed.

"What's going on?" Med asked.

"We were given a chance to relax and hang out somewhere," Cyset said, smiling. "I thought I'd take us to Dave and Don's here in Nexi Sciene."

Med's face lit up. She had heard about this arcade/hangout spot multiple times and had always wanted to go.

"You mean D&D's?" she asked.

"Is that what people call it?" Cyset questioned.

"Well, yeah. It's easier to say."

"Hmm." Cyset sniffed. "Anyway, you in? It's in the heart of the city, in Nomura Square off the corner of Enix Street."

Med was almost bouncing up and down at the idea. "Hell, yeah, I wanna go!"

Cyset smiled.

Med looked sheepish. "Uh, just pretend I said yes."

Cyset raised his hand, stopping her. "Too late. I already heard it, and you can't make me forget."

Med was embarrassed but still happy.

"I'll give you some time to get ready. Just meet me in the garage so we can pick cars."

Before he could walk away, she grabbed his arm. "Wait." Med let go when he turned around. "Why did you become a Mystic?" she asked, looking him in his golden eyes.

Cyset looked up at the ceiling, and Med waited, hoping the question wasn't too personal.

"I only asked because—"

"I wanted to see Mystian," Cyset said.

"You what?"

"I just wanted to see Mystian. If I had just stayed here with Solaria, as her adoptive son, I would have spent all my life in training facilities, pushing the boundaries of magic. As a Mystic, I wouldn't be forced to do that."

"You did this because you wanted to see what the world looks like?" Med asked.

"Oh, I had seen the world before. I had been around to most of the major Mage sites like Rya Drea and a few areas where Mages aren't prevalent, but also the huge cities like Nexi Sciene. Thing was, I was always with Solaria, so I was seeing the picture-perfect version of everywhere I went. I always saw it with a tour guide, and I wanted to do it on my own."

Med was amazed. She had definitely expected Cyset to become a Mystic, but she never thought his reason would be the same as hers. It seemed like he had total freedom, or at the very least, some freedom.

"I guess I thought you were born to be a Mystic," Med said.

"Well, I mean, there's a lot expected of me," Cyset said. "I'm expected to succeed Solaria, and I'm expected to be one of the next great Sorcerers. I just thought being a Mystic was the best way to prepare for it."

Med looked at her friend and smiled. His confidence was infectious. He was someone to talk to, and for the first time in her life, someone who could teach her something useful.

"Hey, can I ask: what was your first impression of me?"

Cyset took a moment. "I kind of thought you were a bit different."

Med stared him down, interrogating him with a look. "Different, meaning…?"

"Meaning you had a more interesting experience. I like to think that may be true." Cyset smiled. "Though I will say I think you have a great chance of being right up there with the rest of us. We just need to make sure you aren't left to fail."

Med was in shock. This compliment was bigger than any she had ever received. She just stood in silence for a moment, and after a while, she responded.

"I, oh… thank you." Med composed herself. "That means a lot."

"Hey, nothing but the truth out of me. Ask a question and I'll answer it. Now, get ready and meet us in the garage. Trust me, you don't want to miss any of this." Cyset walked down the hall.

Med closed the door and scurried through every part of her closet for clothes to wear. She wasn't going to hide; she wanted to look cool. She rummaged through everything until she found a new dark purple tank top and some good jeans to wear. She thought it looked nice and threw it on with her favorite pair of sneakers.

She walked out over to the garage and found the others waiting, all dressed nicer than usual. She smiled from ear to ear. It was nice to see her friends all waiting for her.

"Hey, you look good," Shade said.

"I feel good," Med said.

"Glad to hear it," Dixie added.

"So, we just gonna sit here giving each other compliments, or are we going to have some fun?" Jacks asked.

Med hopped into Dixie's truck along with Scratch. She was absolutely joyful and, for the first time in her life, completely free. Med beamed as she headed to Nomura Square with her friends for a little R&R at D&D's.

CHAPTER 22

D&D'S

Pulling into Nomura Square was a blast for Med. The city's holographic advertisements and the sidewalks were aglow with bright color. The square was filled with people. It was lively; the peak of science and innovation at its finest. Med stared at everything. The allure of the world, the many signs lit up—it was incredible. The vigor of the Square was enough to outdo and outpace Soliopolis on its own. Med would have stared forever if she hadn't been grabbed by the arm.

"Yo, you coming?" Cyset asked, pointing to the entrance of Dave and Don's.

"Of course, I am." Med followed him to the front where the other Mystics were waiting. She saw them looking up at a brightly-colored sign that had a bunch of knights, lancers, and elves running around the fancy words.

"A little much, don't you guys think?" Jacks asked.

"What, like the big flame insignia on the back of your jacket isn't a little much?" Shade asked.

"Nah, nah, that is my signature," Jacks replied, puffing out the jacket.

"It's on the palms of your hands, dude. It's a bit much," Shade said.

"Look, you can make fun of Jacks' choice in clothing later," Cyset joked. "For now, let's just make fun of who plays video games the worst."

Med followed her team leader through to the door into the wonderful world of D&D's.

Inside of Dave and Don's, Med had the time of her life. She looked around at the beautiful lights and huge machines with games and prizes stacked everywhere. Over to her right were some bowling lanes, a VR experience, a floating car course below the glass floor, and a ton of seating areas. She felt like she was getting to catch up on nineteen missed years of nights out. A small tap on her shoulder got her back into reality and she turned to see Shade smiling at her.

"Whoa, don't go all zombie on us," Shade said. "Last thing we need is to lose you in a crowd in this place."

Med rubbed the back of her head. "Sorry, sorry. I got really excited."

"I don't blame you," Shade replied.

Med received a pat on the back as she walked with her friend over to a huge machine where the other Mystics were. Med came in and was handed a card from Cyset.

"All right, here's your game card," he said.

Med pulled it out of his hands and tried to make a joke. "What would your orders be, sir?"

"My orders are to have fun," Cyset returned, laughing.

"Hey, hey!" Jacks shouted. "Yo, I got an idea. Scratch, you're going to drive a virtual car." Jacks pointed to the racing machine.

"Oh, watch me," Scratch challenged, bouncing over.

"Oh, jeez," Cyset wheezed.

Med watched as Jacks put Scratch's card in for him and let him go nuts. She burst out laughing as Scratch drove through every part of the environment, practically crashing through fences and farmland. He broke through a barn and rampaged through a vast area causing incredible amounts of damage in the virtual environment. Med had tears streaming down her eyes at the ridiculous driving Scratch was doing.

Scratch's game continued until he finally finished the race.

Med gave him a small clap with her friends but was still absolutely in hysterics at the whole ordeal.

"Oh, boy, that was amazing," Dixie said.

"I don't know whether I should laugh or be very concerned," Shade gasped, leaning on Dixie.

Med saw Cyset move over to a small test-your-strength machine. "Jacks, what's your record on these punching things?" he asked.

"Last I checked, like 750," Jacks said.

Med watched Cyset swipe his card in the machine and let the punching bag come down. Cyset hit it hard and watched the numbers click up. They landed on 789.

"Oh, no, don't you dare try that," Jacks said. Walking up and punching in his card, Jacks took a swing that ended with 789 as well. Dixie walked over and took a swing, managing to get 950.

"How's that?" Dixie asked.

Med chuckled as she looked at Jacks and Cyset's shocked expressions. She turned and found a claw machine and walked over. The small armadillo plushie made her smile.

"Oh, I want that," Med said.

She swiped her card and went immediately for the plushie once the crane was in motion. She made the claw drop, it grabbed the plushie, and pulled it to the dropbox where Med grabbed her new treat with glee. She squeezed it tight, turning to see the other Mystics staring at her.

"How the hell did you do that?" Shade asked.

"Do what?" Med asked.

"You won a crane game," Jacks said. "I know crane operators who can't win crane games."

"I guess I've got skills," Med replied, squeezing her armadillo plush.

She didn't care if it was luck or not; she was enjoying herself and having fun. Living like a little kid in a never-ending candy store, free and unrestricted. Instead of being stuck on a remote beach, she was having fun in the city. She jumped around with them, explored with them, and laughed with them all throughout the night. Her fun couldn't be stopped for anyone or anything.

"So, how do you feel?" Cyset asked her.

Med took a moment to think and looked up at the sky, her heart full, her world expanded, and her joy immeasurable. She knew exactly what to say.

"Like I'm seeing the world in a new light."

ACKNOWLEDGMENTS

Writing *New Light* was an incredible experience, and the process was helped along by a plethora of people. First and foremost, I want to thank my mother and father, Wayne and Renia Dotson, both of whom helped bring the book to life. I'd also like to thank my younger sister, Mikayla Dotson, who wished me luck and was present at a few writing sessions. Thank you, Shelby, and Morris Morrow, for being the first people to speak about the book and make it known to others.

Thank you to my extended family for jumping onboard by donating and campaigning alongside me. Thanks to Ethan for being incredibly vocal about it. Thank you, Aunt Marilyn, for grabbing more than one copy. Thank you to Justin, Uncle Walter, Nana, Aunt Serena, Aunt Wanda, Aunt Eddye, and Aunt Luci for all being incredibly supportive and bragging any chance you had.

Special thanks to my classmates and professors from Emerson College. Thank you to Hunter Logan for being one of my fellow supporters. Thank you to Jehan Ayesha and Katharine Hanifen for being beta readers. Thank you, Professor Alyson Gamble, for helping me make sure I knew exactly what I was getting into when publishing.

Thank you to members of the Progressive Arts and Civic Club in Greenville, Mississippi. Dr. Nelson, Janice Jelks, Mrs. Leonia Dorsey, and Mrs. Mary Hardy, thank you all for your support and mentorship when I was younger.

Thank you to Levi Satcher, Rashenda Branch, P. Renee Phillips, and especially Dr. James Herzog.

Finally, a big thank you to New Degree Press for helping get this book published. Thank you to Kelly Coons, one of my fellow writers who joined the author community and worked with me extensively on my book. Lastly, thank you to Professor Eric Koester for getting me into the Author Institute and reaching out with the chance to write this book and have it published.